T. B. Peterson

Life and Public Services of Major-General Meade

the hero of Gettysburg, and commander of the Army of the Potomac

T. B. Peterson

Life and Public Services of Major-General Meade
the hero of Gettysburg, and commander of the Army of the Potomac

ISBN/EAN: 9783337196004

Printed in Europe, USA, Canada, Australia, Japan

Cover: Foto ©Raphael Reischuk / pixelio.de

More available books at **www.hansebooks.com**

LIFE AND PUBLIC SERVICES

OF

MAJOR-GENERAL MEADE.

(GEORGE GORDON MEADE.)

THE

HERO OF GETTYSBURG;

AND

COMMANDER OF THE ARMY OF THE POTOMAC.

With a full History of his Life, and Services to his country in all the various positions he has filled, from the time he first entered the United States Army, in 1835, until the present day, with his Official Reports to the War Department, Speeches. etc.

PHILADELPHIA:

T. B. PETERSON & BROTHERS,

306 CHESTNUT STREET.

CONTENTS

(19)

LIFE AND PUBLIC SERVICES

OF

MAJOR-GENERAL MEADE.

—————+•••+•————

HIS BIRTH AND PARENTAGE.

FEW commanders of the Union army have, during the progress of the rebellion, been brought more prominently before the country, or have labored more zealously and heroically in the great cause for which the freemen of the North and West are contending, than GENERAL GEORGE GORDON MEADE, a citizen, of whom Pennsylvania is justly proud, and a patriot, whose worth the country acknowledges and admires. His parents, Richard Worsam Meade and Margaret Butler Meade, were at the time of his birth temporary sojourners in Cadiz, Spain. The father, who was born in 1778, and who had been a successful merchant in Philadelphia, crossed the Atlantic in the early part of the year eighteen hundred, and for several years held the responsible positions of Consul and Navy Agent at Cadiz. The mother of George Meade was a native of Chester county, Pennsylvania, and was descended from an aristocratic family of the South of Ireland, a branch of the race of the Marquises (and former Dukes) of Ormonde, who derived their name from their office of Hereditary Lord High Butlers of Ireland, one of the seven chief officers of the monarch in feudal times.

Mr. Richard W. Meade had been engaged in numerous mercantile transactions with the Spanish Government, and by his probity had secured the confidence of that power to an extent which admirably fitted him for the offices to which he was selected by the President of the United States, and it was mainly by his influence and exertions that the Territory of Florida was acquired, an extended area which at the time included an important portion of Southern Alabama. Indeed, so highly was he appreciated by King Ferdinand, that that monarch withheld for nearly two years his assent to the ratification of the treaty, insisting that a clause should be inserted in the document, acknowledging the services of Mr. Meade in securing the settlement of the mutual claims of the two Governments for spoliations on commerce, and other difficulties growing out of the embarrassed foreign relations of Spain, during the period when Great Britain and France made that country a field of carnage.

HIS EARLY EDUCATION—HE ENTERS WEST POINT.

On the thirty-first of December, 1815, the subject of our sketch was born, and when an infant was brought by his parents to Philadelphia. At an early age he was sent to a school in Georgetown, District of Columbia, where he remained for some time under the preceptorial care of Mr. Salmon P. Chase, now the Honorable Secretary of the Treasury, but who then was known only as a worthy teacher of considerable ability and talent. From Mr. Chase's school he was transferred to a Military Academy at Mount Airy, near Philadelphia, and in September, 1831, had his name inscribed upon the roll at West Point as a cadet. On the first of July, 1835, having graduated on the previous day, in a class which numbered among its members, Naglee, Morell, Martindale, Haupt, Roberts-

and others, who have since acquired distinction as Generals, he entered the army as Brevet Second Lieutenant of the Third Artillery, and was immediately ordered to Florida. During his campaign in that State, he performed valuable service, and was only saved from being a victim in the horrible "Dade Massacre" by an attack of illness, which prevented his serving with his regiment at the time.

RESIGNS THE ARMY AND BECOMES A CIVIL ENGINEER.

He became a full Second Lieutenant on the last day of December of the same year, and in the latter part of October, 1836, resigned his connection with the service, and becoming a Civil Engineer, was employed on various private and Government surveys, the principal one on which his abilities were called into requisition, being the survey of the Northeastern Boundary Line, then under the charge of Colonel James D. Graham, of the Topographical Engineers.

RE-ENTERS THE ARMY—HIS CAREER IN MEXICO.

On the nineteenth day of May, 1842, he was re-appointed in the army as Second Lieutenant of the Topographical Engineers. Soon after the commencement of hostilities between the United States and Mexico, Lieutenant Meade received orders to proceed to the seat of war, and during that campaign gave the first evidence of those superior military traits and qualifications which have since made him so renowned. As a member, at different periods, of the staff of Generals Taylor, Patterson and Worth, his usefulness was found invaluable, while in every engagement in which he participated—Palo Alto, Resaca de la Palma, Monterey and Saltillo—his conduct was marked by a degree of bravery which made him the recipient of

commendations from his commanding officers. At Palo
Alto he particularly distinguished himself, and for gallantry
during the memorable siege of Monterey was brevetted a
First Lieutenant. During the siege of Vera Cruz he also
rendered valuable service, having, as the Topographical
Engineer on the staff of Major-General Patterson, made
several important reconnoissances, and also selected the
site for the Naval battery. After the siege had successfully terminated, Lieutenant Meade returned to the United
States, strongly recommended for promotion. His valor
was appreciated by the people of the Union, as well as by
his superior officers and military associates, and after his
arrival in Philadelphia he was presented with a costly
sword, as a slight token of the estimation in which he was
held by his fellow-citizens.

IS AGAIN ORDERED TO FLORIDA—FORT MEADE.

After the declaration of peace he was actively employed
on River and Harbor improvements, and in the construction of light houses, principally in Delaware Bay, but
upon hostilities being again threatened in Florida, he re-
linquished these peaceable pursuits and again took the
field with his old commander, General Zachary Taylor.

He remained in Florida about six months, and among
other incidents related of him during that campaign, is the
following:—General Twiggs, desirous of selecting an ad-
vantageous site for a fort on the western coast of the
State, consulted Lieutenant Meade in the matter, but subsequently discarded his recommendations and accepted
those of a civilian. Subsequent events convinced him of
his error, and not only did he construct a fortification on
Pease Creek, south of Tampa Bay, in accordance with the
suggestion of the young officer, but as an additional evidence of his confidence in his adviser, ordered it to be designated Fort Meade, a title it bears to the present day

RETURNS TO LIGHT HOUSE DUTY—SURVEYS THE NORTHWESTERN LAKES.

The war ended, he again returned to the responsible duty of superintending the erection of light houses, not only in Delaware Bay, of which District he had been placed in charge, but also off the coast of the State in which but a short time before he had wielded the sword. In August, 1851, he became a First Lieutenant, and on the nineteenth of May, 1856, a Captain.

In the latter year he was ordered to Détroit, Michigan, to assist in prosecuting the National Survey of the Great Western and Northwestern Lakes, of which important work he soon after was selected to take charge. Under his practised eye and able supervision, the work progressed rapidly and satisfactorily, and the various charts of the Lake district and reports of the surveys, bear flattering testimony to the admirable manner in which the duty was performed. His services were acknowledged and received their meed of praise at Washington, while his many noble and gentlemanly qualities won for him the esteem of the people of Detroit, and indeed of every city and town on the Northern border, where, in the prosecution of his official labors, he was a transient visitor.

IS APPOINTED BRIGADIER-GENERAL AND ORDERED TO THE PENNSYLVANIA RESERVES.

When the rebellion broke out, Captain Meade was still at Detroit, but was immediately ordered to report at Washington, and on the thirty-first of August, 1861, he received the appointment of Brigadier-General of Volunteers, and was assigned to the command of the Second Brigade of that noble organization, the Pennsylvania Reserve Corps, which with prudent foresight had been raised in the Keystone State, and placed under the command of General McCall.

HIS SERVICES WITH McDOWELL AND ON THE PENINSULA.

He assumed the command on the 13th of September, 1861, at Tenallytown, near Georgetown, District of Columbia, and during the following winter remained at that place, superintending the drilling of his men and preparing them for the arduous labors, which in the future they would be called upon to accomplish. When the order to advance to Manassas was given to the Army of the Potomac, in the spring of 1862, the Reserves took up their line of march as one of the three Divisions of the First Corps, then under the command of General McDowell, and with that officer they remained until after the Battle of Hanover Court-House, when they were ordered to join General McClellan on the Peninsula, and upon their arrival were constituted a part of the Fifth Corps, on the right wing, with head-quarters in the vicinity of Mechanicsville. During their connection with General McDowell, the Second Brigade made one or more reconnoissances, the most important of which was one made in December, under the leadership of General Meade, from their encampment in Fairfax county to a point near Drainesville, during which they secured a large amount of supplies. Later in the same month, while the Battle of Drainesville was progressing, the Second Brigade was ordered to support General Ord's Brigade, which was engaging the enemy, but although General Meade promptly brought forward his command, their services were made unnecessary by the rout of the enemy.

On the nineteenth of June, 1862, the distinguished subject of our sketch was promoted to the rank of a Major in the regular army.

During his campaign on the Peninsula, he acquired additional celebrity for bravery and gallantry, and in the various engagements in which his Brigade participated, by his courage and heroism stimulated his followers to the accomplishment of deeds which have reflected credit and renown upon his command, and honor upon the Commonwealth, of which they were such faithful and chivalrous representatives.

HIS SERVICES IN THE BATTLES OF MECHANICSVILLE AND GAINES'S MILLS.

On the 26th of June, 1862, was fought the Battle of Mechanicsville, the first of the series of engagements known as the "Seven Days' Contests." General McCall held the Second Brigade in reserve in front of Gaines's Farm, ready to act either in support of the First and Third Brigades, or to oppose the crossing at New Bridge, should it be attempted. About noon the enemy was discovered advancing, and in a short time the pickets of the Reserves were driven in, and not long afterwards the head of the column appeared in front of Mechanicsville. Meade's Brigade had in the meantime been ordered to occupy a position in the rear of the line, where it would be out of musketry range, and yet within supporting distance. During the engagement that followed, the men of the Second fought valiantly, while their commander's noble conduct was particularly noticed. At an early hour of the twenty-seventh, General McCall was ordered to withdraw his Division and fall back to the rear of Gaines's Mills. Meade's Brigade was the first withdrawn, and while the men were retiring, the enemy opened a fire which was promptly returned. The Brigade, however, retired in excellent order, and for his action during the day, General Meade received the thanks of his commanding officer.

On the following day, General Meade's services were again called into requisition. The Division had arrived in the rear of Gaines's Mills at ten o'clock in the morning, and soon after the battle commenced in the afternoon, the Second and Third Brigades were ordered to support our first line, a command which was obeyed with such alacrity as to receive the praise of the Commanding General. These two Brigades were soon engaged, as was also the remaining Brigade, and for three hours the gallant Reserves contended manfully against the army of determined traitors. One regiment, the Fourth, was compelled to succumb to overpowering numbers, but being rallied by General Meade, resumed position in line of battle; and for this and other valuable assistance afforded during the hard-fought battle, he again received the thanks of General McCall, and was nominated for the Brevet of Lieutenant Colonel.

THE BATTLE OF NEW-MARKET CROSS-ROADS, OR GLENDALE—GENERAL MEADE BADLY WOUNDED.

On the evening of the Battle of Gaines's Mills, the Reserves crossed the Chickahominy to Trent's Hill, where they remained until the evening of the following day, when they moved to the crossing of White Oak creek, arriving at noon of the twenty-ninth. Five hours later they advanced to the Quaker road crossing of the New-Market road, and took a position to repel an attack from the direction of Richmond. They were subsequently ordered to return, and at seven o'clock on the morning of the thirtieth, halted at the junction of the New-Market and Turkey Bridge roads, where they halted with instructions to repel any attack the enemy might make upon the immense supply-trains of the army, which were then passing towards the James river. General McCall, in placing his troops, posted General Meade's Brigade on the right, and awaited the approach of the rebels. About half-past two P.M., the pickets were driven in, and half an hour later the enemy advanced a regiment on the left centre,

and one on the right, but both were driven back, the former by the Third Regiment, and the latter by the Seventh,
both belonging to the Second Brigade.   Soon afterwards
the battle raged with almost unexampled fierceness, the
enemy not unfrequently advancing to the muzzles of our
cannon.   General Meade's commanding figure was seen
wherever and whenever the fray was the hottest, and such
was his coolness that while the shot and shell were falling
around him, he calmly took a segar from his pocket, and
lighting it, enjoyed the luxury, while at the same time he
issued his various orders.

A correspondent of one of the newspapers of the day
thus describes the conclusion of the battle :

"We are all anxious, eagerly expectant. Easton's battery, seen
a few rods above, with the Fourth regiment of Reserves, the
guns unlimbered, the cannoniers waiting the signal, while the
captain is anxiously looking for the appearance of the enemy.
Further below us is a ravine, and sharp eyes think that they can
see glistening bayonets and the movement of a line of black
caps.   General Meade sends an order to the captain to throw a
few shells into the ravine.   A moment more and the sharp sound
of artillery breaks upon the ear.   This gives meaning to the
scene, more particularly as we see that line of shining steel and
black caps come up from the ravine, and out of the woods,
moving up the hill slowly, shoulder to shoulder, step keeping
step, and their hateful colors borne above them.   Then they
seemed to see our front, and they began a flank movement, as
it were turning on the rim of a wheel, straggling men keeping
up the line of march, constantly firing.   The battery played
upon them, but it seemed their fire was altogether directed upon
the horses.   The fire became incessant, rapid, and ceaseless;
the rebels drew nearer and nearer.   That steady line of the
Pennsylvania Reserves fired volley after volley, until the air
seemed to be but an echo of reverberating sounds, and the heav-
ens became black with the smoke.   The carnage must have
been fearful.   Gaps appeared in the advancing rebel line, only
to be filled up by new men; and the line steadily marched over
ridges of the dead and dying.   Sixty rounds were fired, and the
regiment retired to obtain ammunition, while another regiment
took its place.   The rebels still came nearer, shots grew
more and more frequent, men became wild with excitement,
officers shouted, the wounded were hastily carried away—
all this time running to and fro and all this in less time than

I have taken to write this line. Still the long line came
nearer, so near that I am confident that, if I should meet with
some of the faces I saw that day in gray uniform, my memory is
distinct enough to enable me to recognize them. No time must
be lost. General Meade rode up, saying, 'Men, you have done
nobly; you have covered yourselves with glory. You could
not have pleased me better.' He asked Colonel Sickels whether
his regiment might not be relieved—whether his men were not
badly cut up. The colonel replied, 'Well, the boys are good
enough for another turn yet.' The general then asked the
colonel if he could not give them a bayonet charge. 'I think
we can,' said the colonel, 'although we are very tired;' and in
a moment more the order was given, 'Charge!' I can think
of nothing to describe this scene. Like a flash of lightning—
the twinkling of an eye—it was but a moment—and all was
over. Along the slope they ran, the men shouting. Pres-
ently the steel grappled. A sharp tussle, a ringing, dull, and
heavy sound—it sounded strangely in the lull of the musketry—
a few more groans of the wounded and dying, and the shout of
triumph broke exultingly upon the ear. The enemy could not
stand the strong arms of the Union soldiers, and they fell back
in dismay, our men rapidly pursuing them. This was, by all
odds, one of the most exciting, briefly contested episodes of the
battle; and the gallantry and coolness exhibited by those engaged in it deserves loftier praise than I could bestow.
" We had accomplished our mission. We had held the rebels
at bay, and prevented them from throwing their force upon
McClellan's exposed column."

Throughout this sanguinary struggle, the Reserves displayed their usual valor, and gained additional and un-
fading laurels. No more convincing proof could be elicited,
or more honorable mention made of the important service
rendered by the Division, than the following extract from
a despatch from General Meade to General McClellan:—
" It was only the stubborn resistance," says the General,
" offered by our Division (the Pennsylvania Reserves),
prolonging the contest till after dark, and checking till that
time the advance of the enemy, that enabled the concentration during the night of the whole army on James
river, which saved it." The enemy fought with unusual
desperation, but could not withstand the determined
charges of our heroes. All fought well, but none in the
Union ranks performed their duty more creditably than

the men of the Second Brigade. The losses of the Division were appalling, and among those who were compelled to leave the field towards the close of the fight, wounded, was General Meade, who, while leading his column, received two balls, one entering his arm, and the other penetrating just above the hip-bone, and passing round the body, made its exit just before reaching the spine. Notwithstanding the severity of the wounds, he rode for some distance to a temporary hospital, where, alighting, he received medical attention, and was then placed in an ambulance and carried to the James river, from whence he was removed to his home in Philadelphia, where he arrived on the morning of the fourth of July. At first his injuries were supposed to be mortal, but God designed the able commander for even more exalted honors than he had achieved in his past brilliant career, and in less than six weeks he had sufficiently recovered to again bid farewell to the loving relations who had surrounded his couch, night and day, during his hours of suffering.

REJOINS HIS BRIGADE—HIS SERVICES UNDER GENERAL POPE.

Proceeding to Harrison's Landing, he rejoined the army on the 13th of August, 1862, and when a few days later that army evacuated the Peninsula to join General Pope, the Pennsylvania Reserve Corps accompanied it. Having arrived at Fredericksburg, the Division was ordered on the twenty-first of August to proceed to Kelly's Ford, on the Rappahannock, and from thence to join the Army of Virginia, then on its march to Warrenton from Rappa? hannock Station. Reaching Warrenton, it was assigned temporarily to General McDowell's Army Corps, and on the twenty-fourth encamped one mile south of that place, with General Meade's brigade two miles in advance. On the twenty-seventh, General John F. Reynolds, in command of the Reserves, moved to Manassas by the way of

Gainesville, and on arriving at the latter place, his command was fired upon by two pieces of the enemy in position on the heights above Groveton, which were immediately replied to by one of our batteries, while General Meade rapidly placed his men in line of battle. The latter met with some loss, but the enemy retired after a brief demonstration. On the following day, General Meade was again actively engaged, and again on each successive day during that never-to-be-forgotten retreat, which closed the celebrated Pope campaign. During the actions of the twenty-eighth, twenty-ninth, and thirtieth of August, General Meade had twelve of his command killed, ninety-six wounded and seventy-seven missing. The casualties in the Division during the three days, numbered six hundred and fifty-three. In the official report of General Reynolds, that officer remarks : " General Meade, as heretofore, led and conducted his brigade in the most skilful manner throughout the entire marches and actions ;" and General Pope thus officially refers to the valor of the Reserves and the efficiency of General Meade : "The Pennsylvania Reserves under Reynolds rendered most gallant and efficient service in all the operations which occurred after they had reported to me. General Meade performed his duty with ability and gallantry, and in all fidelity to the Government and to the army."

TAKES COMMAND OF THE RESERVES—THE BATTLE OF SOUTH MOUNTAIN.

Early in September, 1862, General Meade marched his command with the other gallant and, notwithstanding their disastrous retreat, undaunted troops comprising the Army of the Potomac, towards that portion of Maryland into which Lee with his forces flushed with victory was rapidly advancing. General Reynolds was relieved from the command of the Reserves for the purpose of organizing the militia of Pennsylvania and preparing them for armed resistance to the enemies of their country, and on the twelfth of September, General Meade was ordered to assume his position. In the Battle of South Mountain, as a portion of Hooker's Corps, the veteran Division displayed their usual prowess. Every man was at his post, and notwithstanding the incessant fire, the line moved forward, pouring volley after volley into the enemy's ranks, until victory crowned their efforts. General Hooker's Corps had left their position on the Monocacy creek early in the morning, and reached the Catoctin creek soon after noon, and at one o'clock General Meade's Division was ordered to make a diversion in favor of General Reno, who was then engaging the enemy. The Division left in pursuance to these orders about two o'clock, and turned off to the right from the main road, on the old Hagerstown road, to Mount Tabor Church, and deployed a short distance in advance, its right resting a little more than a mile from the turnpike. A few shots were fired from a rebel battery on the mountain side, but not much damage was effected. The First Pennsylvania Rifles were soon after sent forward as skirmishers, and General Meade was directed to advance his Division to the right of the road, so as to outflank, if possible, the enemy, who were found to be in force, and then to move forward and attack. The ground was of the most difficult character; but, regardless of the natural obstructions and those which by means of stone and timber the rebels had constructed, the Pennsylvania troops marched up the mountain side, gradually dislodging the rebels from their positions. The action became general, and the gallant commander of the Reserves believing that efforts were being made to outflank him, applied for reinforcements, but before they arrived, the enemy, unable to contend against their veteran adversaries, retired, leaving General Meade in possession of the field. The admirable manner in which our hero handled his men

2

and directed their movements, won the commendation of his superior officers and the admiration of his men, who, stimulated by the confidence they had in his ability to lead them to success, clambered up to the crest and drove the foe down the rugged side to the valley beneath. The loss of the Reserves in the engagement, in killed, wounded and missing, was three hundred and ninety-two officers and men.

TUESDAY'S FIGHT AT ANTIETAM CREEK.

On the night of the battle of South Mountain our pickets were advanced and pursuit was commenced, General Hooker's corps marching by the National turnpike and Boonsboro. On the afternoon of the sixteenth, General Hooker was ordered to cross the Antietam creek with his corps to attack, and, if possible, to turn the enemy's left. Upon approaching their pickets, the Union skirmishers were fired upon, and in a short time General Meade's corps was hotly engaged. A battle of a desperate character progressed for nearly four hours, at the end of which time the enemy fled and were pursued by Meade for nearly three miles. The firing continued until after dark, when the weary Pennsylvania troops, who had, unassisted by their comrades belonging to the other divisions of the corps, fought and conquered a greatly superior force, rested upon the battle field.

THE BATTLE OF ANTIETAM—MEADE AND HIS RESERVES.

Exhausted as they were by long marches and the sanguinary engagements they had just passed through, they were not to be permitted to rest long upon their laurels.

At dawn of day on the seventeenth, the great battle of Antietam was commenced by the skirmishers of the Pennsylvania Reserves. The left of General Meade's command and the right of General Rickett's line became engaged

about the same moment, one with artillery, the other with
infantry. An eye-witness thus describes the part the
Reserves took in the fight that followed :

"A battery was almost immediately pushed forward beyond
the central woods, over a ploughed field near the top of the slope
where the cornfield began. On this open field, in the corn
beyond, and in the woods which stretched forward into the
broad fields like a promontory into the ocean, were the hardest
and deadliest struggles of the day. For half an hour after the
battle had grown to its full strength, the line of fire swayed
neither way. The half hour passed ; the rebels began to give
way a little—only a little, but at the first indication of a rece-
ding fire, ' Forward' was the word, and on went the line with a
cheer and a rush. Back across the cornfield, leaving dead and
wounded behind them, over the fence, and across the road, and
then back again into the dark woods which closed around them,
went the retreating rebels. Meade and his Pennsylvanians followed hard and fast—followed till they came within easy range
of the woods, among which they saw their beaten enemy disap-
pearing, followed still with another cheer, and flung themselves
against the cover.
 " But out of those gloomy woods came suddenly and heavily,
terrible volleys—volleys which smote, and bent, and broke in a
moment that eager front and hurled them swiftly back for
half the distance they had won. Not swiftly, or in panic, any
further. Closing up their shattered lines, they came slowly
away ; a regiment where a brigade had been ; hardly a brigade
where a whole division had been victorious. They had met
at the woods the first volleys of musketry from fresh troops—had
met them and returned them till their line had yielded and gone
down before the weight of fire, and till their ammunition was
exhausted."

Pen can never do full justice to that noble body of
veterans for their conduct throughout that memorable
day. At one hour gallantly forcing the enemy back, and
at another themselves compelled to succumb to overpowering masses, they still maintained that firm determination
and exemplary discipline which in former contests had
made them irresistible. Their brave general was constantly cheering and encouraging them with his presence
and his voice, and not content with giving an order, went
himself to see it executed. Shot and shell ploughed the

earth around him, and hundreds of his valorous followers fell within the scope of his vision, but he rode backwards and forwards along his line, apparently without the slightest apprehension of the dangers he encountered. Several of his regiments were terribly cut up, while the entire loss in the division was within two of six hundred. General Meade received a slight contusion from a spent grape shot, and had two horses killed under him.

After General Hooker was wounded, General Meade was placed temporarily in command of his corps, which position he held until the return of General Reynolds from Pennsylvania, when he re-assumed command of the Reserve corps.

IS APPOINTED MAJOR GENERAL OF VOLUN-TEERS.

When the Army of the Potomac again crossed the Potomac in the latter part of October, 1862, General Meade accompanied it, and on the twenty-ninth of the following month (November) was rewarded for his repeated acts of gallantry by an appointment as major-general of volunteers, an honorable promotion for which he had been earnestly recommended by General Hooker. This additional honor was received with great satisfaction not only by the community in which he was more particularly known and esteemed, but by the country at large.

THE BATTLE OF FREDERICKSBURG — GENERAL MEADE'S OFFICIAL REPORT.

At the battle of Fredericksburg in December, 1862, the Reserves were connected with General Reynolds's corps and Franklin's Grand Division, and were among the first to cross the Rappahannock on the night and morning preceding the engagement. Fire being opened upon the Grand Division it was immediately responded to by Generals Meade and Doubleday, who kept the rebel forces at

bay for several hours. Finding that the enemy largely
outnumbered our own forces, reinforcements were sent
for, and when they arrived upon the field they discovered
that the Reserves held the right and were fighting bravely,
as they continued to do until the close of the fearful struggle. About one o'clock, General Meade ordered a charge
up the slope, and leading his men to the assault carried
his colors successfully into the enemy's intrenchments and
captured several hundred prisoners. Unfortunately he
was not reinforced and was compelled by overwhelming
numbers of fresh troops to retrace his steps. The following is the official report of General Meade :

"HEAD-QUARTERS, THIRD DIVISION, FIRST CORPS,
"ARMY OF THE POTOMAC,
"*December* 20th, 1862.

"CAPTAIN : I have the honor to submit the subjoined report
of the part taken by this division in the recent operations in the
vicinity of Fredericksburg.

"This division is composed of three brigades, organized and
commanded as follows :

"The First brigade, Colonel Wm. T. Sinclair, Sixth regi-
ment Pennsylvania Reserve corps, commanding, consists of the
First rifles, (Bucktails,) First, Second, and Sixth regiments
Pennsylvania Reserve corps.

"The Second brigade, commanded by Colonel A. L. Magilton,
Fourth regiment Pennsylvania Reserve corps, contains the Third,
Fourth, Seventh and Eighth regiments Pennsylvania Reserve
corps, together with the One-hundred-and-forty-second regiment Pennsylvania volunteers.

"The Third brigade, commanded by Brigadier-General C.
Feger Jackson, was composed of the Fifth, Ninth, Tenth,
Eleventh and Twelfth regiments Pennsylvania Reserve corps.

"Attached to this division were four batteries, each of four
guns ; two of light 12-pounders, one commanded by Captain D.
R. Ransom, Third United States artillery ; the other by Lieutenant T. G. Simpson, First Pennsylvania artillery ; and two
of 3-inch rifled guns, commanded by Captains J. H. Cooper
and F. P. Amsden, First Pennsylvania artillery.

"On the eleventh instant the division moved from the camp
near White Oak Church to the vicinity of the point on the
Rappahannock river selected for the crossing of the left grand
division. The previous evening, Captain Amsden's battery of
rifled guns had been detached and ordered to report to Captain
De Russy, United States army, for service on the river bank.

Brigadier-General Jackson's brigade, together with Ransom's and Simpson's batteries, were also detached and sent down during the night of the tenth and posted on the river bank to protect the crossing party, which duty was successfully accomplished without any loss, although there was considerable firing between our sharpshooters and those of the enemy posted on the opposite bank.

"The bridges being completed, the division crossed the river on the morning of the twelfth, and was posted on the plateau, on the left of the line of battle formed by the left grand division.

"The following was the formation of the division : The first brigade in line of battle, its left resting on the river bank, and the line extending, in a northwesterly direction, along and in rear of the ravine at Smithfield, the right connecting with the left of Gibbon's division. Two regiments of this brigade, the First rifles and Second infantry, were detached ; the former for picket duty, the latter to occupy the buildings and outhouses at Smithfield, and to hold the bridge across the ravine at its debouche into the river.

"The batteries were posted in front of the First brigade, on the edge of the ravine, where they had complete command of the front and of the approach by the Bowling Green road.

"The Second brigade was formed in line of battle three hundred paces in rear of the First, and parallel to it; and the Third brigade along the river bank in column of regiments, the head of the column being one hundred paces in rear of the left of the Second brigade. This position was occupied by 3 P.M., without any serious opposition from the enemy, but with occasional skirmishes with the pickets in front.

"Early on the morning of the thirteenth, I accompanied the general commanding the First corps to the head-quarters of the left grand division, where the commanding general indicated the point he was instructed to attack ; and I was informed that my division had been selected to make the attack. The point indicated was on the ridge, or rather range of heights, extending from the Rappahannock, in rear of Fredericksburg, to the Massaponax, and was situated near the left of this ridge, where it terminated in the Massaponax valley. Between the heights to be attacked, and the plateau on which the left grand division was posted, there was a depression or hollow of several hundred yards in width, through which, and close to the foot of the heights, the Richmond railroad ran. The heights along the east were wooded. The slope to the railroad from the extreme left, for the space of three hundred or four hundred yards, was clear. Beyond this it was wooded ; the woods extending across the hollow, and in front of the railroad. The plateau on our side was level, and cultivated ground up to the crest of the hollow, where there was quite a fall to the railroad.

"The enemy occupied the wooded heights, the line of the railroad, and the woods in front. Owing to the woods, nothing could be seen of them, while all our movements on the cleared ground were exposed to their view.

"Immediately on receiving orders, the division was moved forward, across the Smithfield ravine, advancing down the river some seven or eight hundred yards, when it turned sharp to the right, and crossed the Bowling Green road, which here runs in a parallel direction with the railroad. Some time was consumed in removing the hedge fences on this road, and bridging the drains on each side for the passage of artillery.

"Between nine and ten o'clock, the column of attack was formed, as follows: The First brigade in line of battle on the crest of the hollow, and facing the railroad, with the Sixth regiment deployed as skirmishers; the Second brigade in rear of the First three hundred paces; the Third brigade by the flank, its right flank being a few yards to the rear of the First brigade, having the Ninth regiment deployed on its flank as skirmishers and flankers; the batteries between the First and Second brigades.

"This disposition had scarcely been made when the enemy opened a brisk fire from a battery posted on the Bowling Green road, the shot from which took the command from the left and rear. Apprehending an attack from that quarter, the Third brigade was faced to the left, (thus forming, with the First, two sides of a square.) Simpson's battery was advanced to the front and left of the Third brigade, and Cooper's and Ransom's batteries moved to a knoll on the left of the First brigade. These batteries immediately opened on the enemy's battery, and, in conjunction with some of General Doubleday's batteries in our rear, on the other side of the Bowling Green road, after some twenty minutes' firing, silenced and compelled the withdrawal of the guns.

"During this artillery duel, the enemy advanced a body of sharpshooters along the Bowling Green road, and under cover of the hedges and trees at the roadside. General Jackson promptly sent out two companies of marksmen from his brigade, who drove the enemy back. No further demonstration on our left and rear being made, the advance was again determined on.

"Previous to pushing forward the infantry, the batteries were directed to shell the heights and the woods in front. For this purpose, and to protect our line in case of falling back, Ransom's battery was moved to the right and front of the First brigade, and Amsden's battery, which had just rejoined from detached duty, was posted on the right of Cooper.

"During this operation, by the orders of the general commanding First corps, the Third brigade changed front, and formed in line of battle on the left of the First brigade, its left extending so as to be nearly opposite to the end of the ridge to be attacked. The formation was barely executed before the enemy opened a sharp fire from a battery posted on the heights to our extreme left. Cooper's, Amsden's, and Ransom's batteries were immediately turned on it, and, after about thirty minutes' rapid firing, the enemy abandoned the guns, having had two of his limbers or caissons blown up, the explosions from which were plainly visible. As soon as the enemy's guns were silenced, the line of infantry was advanced to the attack.

" 'The First brigade to the right advanced several hundred yards over cleared ground, driving the enemy's skirmishers before them, till they reached the woods previously described as being in front of the railroad, which they entered, driving the enemy out of them to the railroad, where they were found strongly posted in ditches and behind temporary defences. The brigade (First) drove them from there, and up the heights in their front. Owing to a heavy fire being received on their right flank, they obliqued over to that side, but continued forcing the enemy back till they had crowned the crest of the hill, crossed a main road which runs along the crest, and reached open ground on the other side, where they were assailed by a very severe fire from a large force in their front, and at the same time the enemy opened a battery which completely enfiladed them from the right flank. After holding their ground for some time, and no support arriving, they were compelled to fall back to the railroad.

" 'The Second brigade, which advanced in rear of the First, after reaching the railroad, with so severe a fire on their right flank that the Fourth regiment halted and formed, faced to the right, to repel this attack. The other regiments, in passing through the woods, being assailed from the left, inclined in that direction and ascended the heights, the Third going up as the One-hundred-and-twenty-first of the First brigade was retiring. The Third continued to advance, and reached nearly the same point as the First brigade, but was compelled to withdraw for the same reason. The Seventh engaged the enemy to the left, capturing many prisoners, and a standard, driving them from their rifle-pits and temporary defences, and continuing the pursuit till encountering the enemy's reinforcements, they were, in turn, driven back. The Third brigade had not advanced over one hundred yards when the battery on the height on its left was re-manned, and poured a destructive fire into its ranks. Perceiving this, I despatched my aide-de-camp, Lieutenant Dehon, with orders for General Jackson to move by the right flank till he could clear the open ground in front of the battery, and then, ascending the height through the woods, sweep round to the left and take the battery. Unfortunately, Lieutenant Dehon fell just as he reached General Jackson, and, a short time after, the latter officer was killed. The regiments did, however, partially execute the movement by obliquing to the right, and advanced across the railroad, a portion ascending the heights in their front. The loss of their commander and the severity of the fire, from both artillery and infantry, to which they were subjected, compelled them to withdraw, when those on their right withdrew.

"It will be seen from the foregoing that the attack was, for a time, perfectly successful. The enemy was driven from the railroad, his rifle-pits and breastworks, for over half a mile; over two hundred prisoners were taken, and several standards; when the advanced line encountered the heavy reinforcements of the enemy, who, recovering from the effects of our assault, and perceiving both our flanks unprotected, poured in such a destructive fire from all three directions as to compel the line to fall back, which was conducted without confusion.

"Perceiving the danger of too great penetration of my line without support, I despatched several staff officers both to General Gibbon's command and General Birney's. (whose division had replaced mine at the batteries from whence we advanced) urging an advance to my support—the one on my right, the other to the left. A brigade of Birney's advanced to our relief, just as my men were withdrawn from the woods; and Gibbon's division advanced into the woods on our right, in time to assist materially in the safe withdrawal of my broken line.

"An unsuccessful effort was made to re-form the division in the hollow in front of the batteries. Failing in this, the command was re-formed beyond the Bowling Green road, and marched to the ground occupied the night before, where it was held in reserve till the night of the fifteenth, when we re-crossed the river.

"Accompanying this report is a list giving the names of the killed, wounded, and missing, amounting, in the aggregate, to 1,760. When I report that 4,500 men is a liberal estimate of the strength of the division taken into action, this large loss, being nearly forty per cent., will fully bear me out in the expression of my satisfaction at the good conduct of both officers and men. While I deeply regret the inability of the division, after having successfully penetrated the enemy's line, to remain and hold what had been secured, at the same time I deem their withdrawal a matter of necessity. With one brigade commander killed, another wounded, nearly half their number *hors du combat*, with regiments separated from brigades, and companies from regiments, and all the confusion and disaster incidental to the advance of an extended line through woods and other obstructions, assailed by a heavy fire, not only of infantry, but of artillery, not only in front, but on both flanks, the best troops would be justified in withdrawing without loss of honor.

"The reports of the brigade commanders, herewith submitted, are referred to for details not contained in this report.

"My thanks are due to Colonel W. T. Sinclair, Sixth regiment, and Colonel A. L. Magilton, Fourth regiment, for the manner in which they handled their commands. To Colonel

Sinclair particularly, who had command of the advance during the whole day, and who was severely wounded, I desire to express my obligation for the assistance rendered me.

"To the members of my personal staff, Captain F. C. Baird, assistant adjutant general, Captain A. Coxe, Pennsylvania volunteers, and Lieutenant E. G. Mason, Fifth regiment, aides-de-camp, I tender my thanks for the prompt and fearless manner in which they conveyed my orders to all parts of the field. The loss of Lieutenant Arthur Dehon, Twelfth regiment, my aide, is greatly to be deplored, as he was a young man of high promise, endeared to all that knew him for his manly virtues and amiable character.

"The public service has also to mourn the loss of Brigadier-General C. Feger Jackson, an officer of merit and reputation, who owed his position to his gallantry and good conduct in previous actions.

"Others have fallen of distinguished merit, and there are many of the living whom it will be my pleasure hereafter to bring to the notice of the government for their distinguished acts of gallantry.

"At present I must refer to the reports of brigade and regimental commanders.

"I remain, sir, very respectfully, your obedient servant,
"GEORGE G. MEADE,
"*Major-General Commanding.*
"Captain C. KINGSBURY,
"*Ass't Adj't-Gen'l., Head-quarters First Corps.*"

IS APPOINTED TO THE COMMAND OF THE FIFTH CORPS—HIS FAREWELL TO THE RESERVES.

On the 25th of December, 1862, General Meade was appointed to the command of the Fifth Army Corps, and bade farewell to the Division he had led through so many hard-fought engagements in the following general order:

"HEAD-QUARTERS, THIRD DIVISION, FIRST ARMY CORPS.
"*December 25th*, 1862.
"In accordance with Special Order No. 310, which was issued to the different regiments belonging to the Pennsylvania Reserve volunteer corps, which separates the commanding general from the division, he takes occasion to express to the officers and men that, notwithstanding his just pride at being promoted to a higher command, he experiences a deep feeling of regret at parting from them, with whom he has been so long associated, and to whose services he here acknowledges his indebtedness for whatever of reputation he may have acquired.

"The commanding general will never cease to remember that he belonged to the Reserve corps. He will watch with eagerness for the deeds of fame which he feels sure they will enact under the command of his successors ; and, though sadly reduced in numbers from the casualties of battle, yet he knows the Reserves will always be ready and prompt to uphold the honor and glory of their State.

"GEORGE G. MEADE, *Major-General.*"

Gratified as his old followers were at the elevation, they received with sincere sorrow and regret the order which severed their honorable connection.

During the long period he had been with them as Brigade and Division Commander, he had become endeared to every officer and private of the Reserves. In the hour of battle he had proved himself to be the bravest of the brave, and by his personal gallantry had incited them to deeds unsurpassed in the history of the rebellion.

The modest manner in which he worded his farewell address, giving to them and not to himself all the credit for the acts which had promoted his advancement to more exalted military honors, was appreciated by the veterans he complimented, and added to the regret they already experienced.

THE BATTLE OF CHANCELLORSVILLE.

For a brief period General Meade commanded the Centre Grand Division of the Army ; and when, in the latter part of January, 1863, General Hooker succeeded General Burnside as Commander-in-chief of the Army of the Potomac, General Meade was continued in command of the Fifth Corps ; and on the twenty-seventh of April, when the Army commenced the forward movement on Fredericksburg, the Fifth also struck their tents and accompanied it as a part of the right wing. During that advance, the energy and enterprise of this portion of the army were tested to the utmost extent. Leaving camp at Stoneman's Station at one o'clock in the afternoon of the twenty-seventh, the Fifth Corps marched by the way of Kelley's and Ely's Fords to Chancellorsville, arriving there at ten o'clock on the morning of the thirtieth, a distance of nearly fifty miles, accomplished in less than three days. This included all the halts and rests, including one of ten or twelve hours near Kelley's Ford, while the bridge at that point was being constructed, and other corps were cross-ing. During the advance two large rivers were crossed, and half of the time the rain fell in torrents. The fording of the Rapidan by this corps, with its artillery and trains, with the water waist-deep, was considered one of the most brilliant achievements of that subsequently unfortunate movement. Soon after its arrival at Chancellorsville, it became engaged with the skirmishers of the enemy, and captured their rifle-pits and other temporary works. On Sunday morning, the second of May, the great Battle of Chancellorsville opened in front of General Meade's corps, and one of his Brigades was sent into the woods and fought desperately. Artillery soon commenced playing from both sides, and the engagement became general and terrific. The Second Corps supported the Fifth, and the rebels were driven at every point. Throughout the three days' fearful struggle, General Meade displayed the skill in handling troops, which has always marked his partici-pation in the various engagements of the war ; and when at last General Hooker determined to recross the Rappa-hannock, General Meade covered the retreat, and with his wearied men kept a vigilant guard over the crossing until the rest of the noble army had safely reached the northern bank of the stream.

THE MARYLAND CAMPAIGN — GENERAL MEADE APPOINTED COMMANDER-IN-CHIEF OF THE ARMY OF THE POTOMAC.

During the extended and forced marches from the camp-ing grounds in Virginia, through Maryland into Pennsyl-

vania in the latter days of June, 1863, General Meade's
Corps submitted without complaint to the numerous hard-
ships they were called upon to endure, and left no stragglers to denote the course they had taken in pursuit of the
enemy, who were already ravaging the fertile valleys and
despoiling the citizens of the Keystone State.

Before daylight on the morning of Sunday, the twenty-
eighth of June, General Meade was aroused from his
slumbers while reposing within his tent at Frederick,
Maryland, by a messenger from General Halleck, who
notified him that he had been selected to relieve General
Hooker in command of the Army of the Potomac. The
summons was sudden and unexpected, but the gallant and
tried commander was equal to the emergency. The two
opposing forces were face to face, and a struggle, which
promised to be the most sanguinary of the war, was momentarily threatened. Rising from his humble couch, he
prepared himself for the responsible and delicate duties of
his new position, and issued to the army the following
address :

"HEAD-QUARTERS OF THE ARMY OF THE POTOMAC,
"*June 28th*, 1863.

"By direction of the President of the United States, I do
hereby assume command of the Army of the Potomac. As a
soldier, in obeying this order, an order totally unexpected and
unsolicited, I have no promises or pledges to make. The country looks to this army to relieve it from the devastation and
disgrace of a hostile invasion. Whatever fatigues and sacrifices
we may be called upon to undergo, let us have in view constantly
the magnitude of the interests involved, and let each man de-
termine to do his duty, leaving to an all-controlling Providence
the decision of the contest. It is with just diffidence that I relieve in the command of this army an eminent and accomplished soldier, whose name must ever appear conspicuous in
the history of its achievements ; but I rely upon the hearty
support of my companions in arms to assist me in the discharge
of the duties of the important trust which has been confided to
me.   "GEORGE G. MEADE,
"*Major-General Commanding.*

"S. F. BARSTOW,
   "*Assistant Adjutant-General.*"

General Hooker at the same time thus bade farewell to his troops:

"HEAD-QUARTERS, ARMY OF THE POTOMAC,
"FREDERICK, MD., *June 28th*, 1863.

"In conformity with the orders of the War Department, dated June 27th, 1863, I relinquish the command of the Army of the Potomac. It is transferred to Major-General George G. Meade, a brave and accomplished officer, who has nobly earned the confidence and esteem of the army on many a well-fought field. Impressed with the belief that my usefulness as the commander of the Army of the Potomac is impaired, I part from it, yet not without the deepest emotion. The sorrow of parting with the comrades of so many battles is relieved by the conviction that the courage and devotion of this army will never cease nor fail; that it will yield to my successor, as it has to me, a willing and hearty support. With the earnest prayer that the triumph of its arms may bring successes worthy of it and the nation, I bid it farewell.   "JOSEPH HOOKER,
"*Major-General.*

"S. F. BARSTOW,
"*Acting Adjutant-General.*"

Two days later the following circular was issued:

"HEAD-QUARTERS, ARMY OF THE POTOMAC,
"*June 30th*, 1863.

"The commanding general requests that previous to the engagement, *soon expected with the enemy*, corps and all other commanding officers address their troops, explaining to them the immense issues involved in the struggle. The enemy is now on our soil. The whole country looks anxiously to this army to deliver it from the presence of the foe. Our failure to do so will leave us no such welcome as the swelling of millions of hearts with pride and joy at our success would give to every soldier of the army. Homes, firesides, and domestic altars are involved. The army has fought well heretofore. It is believed that it will fight more desperately and bravely than ever, if it is addressed in fitting terms. Corps and other commanders are authorized to order the instant death of any soldier who fails to do his duty at this hour.   "By command of
"*Major-General* MEADE,
"S. WILLIAMS, *Assistant Adjutant-General.*"

The announcement that General Meade had been appointed to lead the veterans of the Army of the Potomac in the expected battle, was received with general favor throughout the country. Although better known to the army than to the public at large, his reputation was sufficiently extended to make his appointment most acceptable to the relatives and friends of the heroes who comprised his command. They had heard of him in the battles upon the Peninsula, and they had received laudatory accounts of his gallantry at South Mountain, Antietam, Fredericksburg and Chancellorsville. He had been selected by the President purely on account of his superior ability, and the selection was ratified by the soldiery and by the unanimous voice of the people. He had during the war considered that his sole duty was to wield his sword in defence of the Union, and had steadily remained aloof from the political and military controversies which have too frequently marred the harmony which should exist among soldiers battling for the same cause. A Captain at the commencement of the rebellion, he had rapidly advanced to the exalted position of Commander-in-Chief of the Army of the Potomac, and in each and every capacity, as Brigade, Division, or Corps commander, his services were conspicuous, receiving the commendation of his superior officers and reflecting credit upon himself, his State and his country.

But amid the rejoicing at the promotion, apprehensions naturally prevailed that the change had been too long deferred, and that the removal of an old, and the appointment of a new leader might prove disastrous to the cause by the defeat of our forces. The change was made at a critical moment, and in the presence of an enemy of whose movements and intentions but little accurate information could be ascertained. Indeed, General Meade encountered more difficulty in procuring information while in Maryland and Pennsylvania, than his predecessors had ever done while in the inhospitable counties of the Old Dominion. His energies, however, were not to be diminished by the apparent carelessness and lack of spirit which seemed to pervade to a greater or less extent the residents of the section in which he was operating, and hastily forming his plans, he gave orders to his eager forces to advance.

THE BATTLE OF GETTYSBURG—GENERAL MEADE'S OFFICIAL REPORT.

Of the great battle which commenced three days after General Meade assumed command of the army, the official report of that officer gives the following complete description :

"HEAD-QUARTERS, ARMY OF THE POTOMAC,
"*October 1st, 1863.*

"GENERAL: I have the honor to submit herewith a report of the operations of this army during the month of July, including details of the battle of Gettysburg, which have been delayed by failure to receive the reports of the several corps and division commanders, who were severely wounded in battle.

"On the twenty-eighth of June I received orders from the President, placing me in command of the Army of the Potomac.

"The situation of affairs was briefly as follows : The Confederate army, which was commanded by General R. E. Lee, was estimated at over one hundred thousand strong. All that army had crossed the Potomac river, and advanced up the Cumberland valley. Reliable intelligence placed his advance thus : Ewell's corps on the Susquehanna, Harrisburgh, and Columbia; Longstreet's corps at Chambersburgh ; and Hill's corps between that place and Cashtown.

"The twenty-eighth of June was spent in ascertaining the positions and strength of the different corps of the army, but principally in bringing up the cavalry which had been covering the rear of the army in its passage over the Potomac, and to which a large increase had just been made from the force previously attached to the defences of Washington.

"Orders were given on this day to Major-General French, commanding at Harper's Ferry, to move with seven thousand men to occupy Frederick and the line of the Baltimore and Ohio railroad, with the balance of his force, estimated at four thousand, to remove and escort public property to Washington.

"On the twenty-ninth the army was put in motion, and on

the evening of that day it was in position, the left at Emmetsburgh and the right at New-Windsor. Buford's division of
cavalry was on the left flank, with his advance at Gettysburg.
Kilpatrick's division was in the front at Hanover, where he encountered this day General Stuart's Confederate cavalry, which
had crossed the Potomac at Seneca creek, and passing our
right flank, was making its way toward Carlisle, having escaped
Greggs's division, which was delayed in taking position on the
right flank by the occupation of the roads by a column of infantry.

"On the thirtieth the right flank of the army was moved up
to Manchester, the left still being at Emmetsburgh, or in that
vicinity, at which place three corps, First, Eleventh, and Third,
were collected under the orders of Major-General Reynolds.

"General Buford having reported from Gettysburg the appearance of the enemy on the Cashtown road in some force,
General Reynolds was directed to occupy Gettysburg.

"On reaching that place, on the first day of July, General
Reynolds found Buford's cavalry warmly engaged with the
enemy, who had debouched his infantry through the mountains
on Cashtown, but was being held in check in the most gallant
manner by Buford's cavalry. Major-General Reynolds immediately moved around the town of Gettysburg, and advanced
on the Cashtown road, and without a moment's hesitation deployed his advanced division and attacked the enemy, at the
same time sending orders for the Eleventh corps, General Howard, to advance as promptly as possible.

"Soon after making his dispositions for attack, Major-General
Reynolds fell mortally wounded, the command of the First corps
devolving on Major-General Doubleday, and the command of
the field on Major-General Howard, who arrived about this
time (half-past eleven A.M.) with the Eleventh corps, then commanded by Major-General Schurz. Major-General Howard
pushed forward two divisions of the Eleventh corps to support
the First corps, now warmly engaged with the enemy on the
north of the town, and posted his third division, with three batteries of artillery, on the Cemetery ridge, on the south side of
the town.

"Up to this time the battle had been with the forces of the
enemy debouching from the mountains on the Cashtown road,
known to be Hill's corps. In the early part of the action the
success was on the enemy's side. Wadsworth's division of the
First corps having driven the enemy back some distance, captured numerous prisoners, among them General Archer, of the
Confederate army.

"The arrival of reinforcements to the enemy on the Cashtown
road, and the junction of Ewell's corps coming in on the York
and Harrisburgh roads, which occurred between one and two
o'clock P.M., enabled the enemy to bring vastly superior forces
against both the First and Eleventh corps, outflanking our line

3

of battle, and pressing it so severely that, about four o'clock
P.M., Major-General Howard deemed it prudent to withdraw
these two corps to the Cemetery ridge, on the south side of the
town, which operation was successfully accomplished—not, however, without considerable loss in prisoners, arising from the confusion incident to portions of both corps passing through the
town, and the men getting confused in the streets.

"About the time of the withdrawal, Major-General Hancock
arrived, whom I had despatched to represent me on the field, on
hearing of the death of General Reynolds. In conjunction with
Major-General Howard, General Hancock proceeded to post the
troops on Cemetery ridge, and to repel an attack that the enemy
made on our right flank. This attack was not, however, very
vigorous; the enemy, seeing the strength of the position occupied, seemed to be satisfied with the success he had accomplished, desisting from any further attack this day.

"About seven o'clock P.M. Major-General Slocum and Sickles,
with the Twelfth corps and part of the Third, reached the
ground and took post on the right and left of the troops previously posted. Being satisfied, from reports received from the
field, that it was the intention of the enemy to support, with his
whole army, the attack already made, and reports from Major-
Generals Hancock and Howard on the character of the position
being favorable, I determined to give battle at this point, and
early in the evening first issued orders to all corps to concentrate at Gettysburg, directing all trains to be sent to the rear
at Westminster at eleven P.M. first.

" I broke up my head-quarters, which till then had been at
Taneytown, and proceeded to the field, arriving there at one A.M.
of the second. So soon as it was light I proceeded to inspect
the position occupied, and to make arrangements for posting
several corps as they should reach the ground.

" By seven A.M. the Second and Fifth corps, with the rest of
the Third, had reached the ground, and were posted as follows:
The Eleventh corps retained its position on Cemetery ridge, just
opposite to the town; the First corps was posted on the right;
the Eleventh on an elevated knoll connecting with the ridge and
extending to the south and east, on which the Twelfth corps was
placed, the right of the Twelfth corps resting on a small stream
at a point where it crossed the Baltimore pike, and which formed
on the right flank of the Twelfth something of an obstacle.

" Cemetery ridge extended in a westerly and southerly direction, gradually diminishing in elevation till it came to a very
prominent ridge called 'Round Top,' running east and west.
The Second and Third corps were directed to occupy the con-
tinuation of Cemetery ridge, on the left of the Eleventh corps
and Fifth corps; pending their arrival the Sixth corps was
held in reserve. While these dispositions were being made, the

enemy was massing his troops on an exterior ridge, distant from the line occupied by us from a mile to a mile and a half.

"At two P.M. the Sixth corps arrived, after a march of thirty-two miles, which was accomplished from nine P.M. of the day previous. On its arrival being reported, I immediately directed the Fifth corps to move over to our extreme left, and the Sixth to occupy its place as a reserve for the right.

"About three P.M. I rode out to the extreme left to await the arrival of the Fifth corps and post it, when I found that Major-General Sickles, commanding the Third corps, not fully apprehending my instructions in regard to the position to be occupied, had advanced, or rather was in the act of advancing his corps some half-mile or three-quarters of a mile in the front of the line of the Second corps on a prolongation which it was designed his corps should rest.

" Having found Major-General Sickles, I was explaining to him that he was too far in the advance, and discussing with him the propriety of withdrawing, when the enemy opened upon him with several batteries in his front and his flank, and immediately brought forward columns of infantry, and made a vigorous assault. The Third corps sustained the shock most heroically. Troops from the Second corps were immediately sent by Major-General Hancock to cover the right flank of the Third corps, and soon after the assault commenced.

"The Fifth corps most fortunately arrived, and took a position on the left of the Third, Major-General Sykes commanding, immediately sending a force to occupy ' Round Top' ridge, where a most furious contest was maintained, the enemy making desperate but unsuccessful efforts to secure it. Notwithstanding the stubborn resistance of the Third corps, under Major-General Birney, (Major-General Sickles having been wounded early in the action,) superiority in numbers of corps of the enemy enabling him to outflank its advanced position, General Birney was counselled to fall back and re-form, behind the line originally desired to be held.

" In the meantime, perceiving the great exertions of the enemy, the Sixth corps, Major-General Sedgwick, and part of the First corps, to which I had assigned Major-General Newton, particularly Lockwood's Maryland brigade, together with detachments from the Second corps, were all brought up at different periods, and succeeded, together with a gallant resistance of the Fifth corps, in checking and finally repulsing the assault of the enemy, who retired in confusion and disorder about sunset, and ceased any further efforts on our extreme left.

"An assault was, however, made about eight P.M. on the Eleventh corps, from the left of the town, which was repelled by the assistance of troops from the Second and First corps. During the heavy assault upon our extreme left, portions of the Twelfth corps were sent as reinforcements.

" During their absence the line on the extreme right was held by a very much reduced force. This was taken advantage of by the enemy, who, during the absence of Geary's division of the Twelfth corps, advanced and occupied part of the line.

" On the morning of the third July, General Geary having returned during the night, attacked at early dawn the enemy and succeeded in driving him back and re-occupying his former position. A spirited contest was maintained all the morning along this part of the line. General Geary, reinforced by Wheaton's brigade of the Sixth corps, maintained his position and inflicted very severe losses on the enemy.

" With this exception, our lines remained undisturbed till one P.M. on the third, when the enemy opened from over one hundred and twenty-five guns, playing upon our centre and left. This cannonade continued for over two hours, when, our guns failing to make any reply, the enemy ceased firing, and soon his masses of infantry became visible, forming for an assault on our left and left centre.

"An assault was made with great firmness, directed principally against the point occupied by the Second corps, and was repelled with equal firmness by the troops of that corps, supported by Doubleday's division and Stannard's brigade of the First corps. During this assault both Major-General Hancock, commanding the left centre, and Brigadier-General Gibson, commanding the Second corps, were severely wounded.

" This terminated the battle, the enemy retiring to his lines, leaving the field strewed with his dead and wounded, and numerous prisoners in our hands.

" Buford's division of cavalry, after its arduous service at Gettysburg, on the first, was, on the second, sent to Westminster to refit and guard our trains. Kilpatrick's division, that on the twenty-ninth, thirtieth, and first had been successfully engaging the enemy's cavalry, was, on the third, sent out on our extreme left, on the Emmetsburgh road, where good service was rendered in assaulting the enemy's line and occupying his attention.

"At the same time General Gregg was engaged with the enemy on our extreme right, having passed across the Baltimore pike and Bonaughtown roads, and boldly attacked the enemy's left and rear.

" On the morning of the fourth, the reconnoissances developed that the enemy had drawn back his left flank, but maintained his position in front of our left, apparently assuming a new line parallel to the mountain.

" On the morning of the fifth it was ascertained that the enemy was in full retreat by the Fairfield and Cashtown roads. The Sixth corps was immediately sent in pursuit on the Fairfield road, and the cavalry on the Cashtown road, and by Emmetsburgh and Monterey passes.

"The fifth and sixth of July were employed in succoring the wounded and burying the dead.

"Major-General Sedgwick, commanding the Sixth corps, having pushed on in pursuit of the enemy as far as Fairfield Pass in the mountains, and reporting that pass as very strong, and one in which a small force of the enemy could hold in check and delay for a considerable time any pursuing force, I determined to follow the enemy by a flank movement, and accordingly leaving McIntosh's brigade of cavalry and Neill's brigade of infantry to continue harassing the enemy, I put the army in motion for Middletown, Maryland.

"Orders were immediately sent to Major-General French, at Frederick, to re-occupy Harper's Ferry, and to send a force to occupy Turner's Pass, in South-Mountain. I subsequently ascertained that Major-General French had not only anticipated these orders in part, but had pushed his cavalry force to Williamsport and Falling Waters, where they destroyed the enemy's pontoon-bridge and captured its guard. Buford was at the same time sent to Williamsport and Hagerstown.

"The duties above assigned to the cavalry was most successfully accomplished, the enemy being greatly harassed, his trains destroyed, and many captures in guns and prisoners made. After halting a day at Middletown to procure necessary supplies and to bring up trains, the army moved through South-Mountain, and by the twelfth of July was in front of the enemy, who occupied a strong position on the heights of Marsh Run, in advance of Williamsport.

"In taking this position, several skirmishes and affairs had been had with the enemy, principally by cavalry, from the Eleventh and Sixth corps.

"The thirteenth was occupied in making reconnoissances of the enemy's position and preparations for attack, but on advancing on the morning of the fourteenth, it was ascertained he had retired the night previous by a bridge at Falling Waters and a ford at Williamsport.

"The cavalry in pursuit overtook the rear-guard at Falling Waters, capturing two guns and numerous prisoners.

"Previous to the retreat of the enemy, Gregg's division of cavalry had crossed at Harper's Ferry, and coming up with the rear of the enemy at Charlestown and Shepherdstown, had a spirited contest, in which the enemy were driven to Martinsburgh and Winchester, and pressed and harassed in his retreat.

"Pursuit was resumed by a flank movement of the army, crossing the Potomac at Berlin, and moving down Loudon Valley. Cavalry were immediately pushed into several passes of the Blue Ridge, and having learned from scouts of the withdrawal of the Confederate army from the lower valley of the Shenandoah, the Third corps, Major-General French in advance, was moved into Manassas Gap, in the hope of being able to intercept a portion of the enemy.

"The possession of the gap was disputed so successfully as to enable the rear-guard to withdraw by way of Strasburgh, the Confederate army retiring to the Rapidan. Position was taken with this army on the line of the Rappahannock, and the campaign terminated about the close of July.

"The result of the campaign may be briefly stated in the defeat of the enemy at Gettysburg, their compulsory evacuation of Pennsylvania and Maryland, and withdrawal from the upper valley of the Shenandoah, and the capture of three guns, forty-one standards, and thirteen thousand six hundred and twenty-one prisoners. Twenty-four thousand nine hundred and seventy-eight small arms were collected on the battle-field.

"Our own losses were very severe, amounting, as will be seen by the accompanying return, to two thousand eight hundred and thirty-four killed, thirteen thousand seven hundred and nine wounded, and six thousand six hundred and forty-three missing —in all twenty-three thousand one hundred and eighty-six.

"It is impossible, in a report of this nature, to enumerate all the instances of gallantry and good conduct which distinguished our success on the hard-fought field of Gettysburg. The reports of corps commanders and their subordinates, herewith submitted, will furnish all information upon this subject.

"I will only add my tribute to the heroic bravery of the whole army, officers and men, which, under the blessing of Divine Providence, enabled the crowning victory to be obtained, which I feel confident the country will never cease to bear in grateful remembrance.

"It is my duty, as well as my pleasure, to call attention to the earnest efforts and co-operation on the part of Major-General D. N. Couch, commanding the department of the Susquehannah, and particularly to his advance of four thousand men under Brigadier-General W. F. Smith, who joined me at Boonsboro', just prior to the withdrawal of the Confederate army.

"In conclusion, I desire to return my thanks to my staff, general and personal, to each and all of whom I was indebted for unremitting activity and most efficient assistance.

" Very respectfully, your obedient servant,
"GEORGE G. MEADE,
"*Major-General Commanding.*
" Brigadier-General L. THOMAS,
Adjutant-General U. S. A."

GENERAL MEADE'S HEAD-QUARTERS UNDER FIRE.

During the greater portion of that terrible fight, General Meade with his staff occupied a little one-story frame house to the left and rear of the beautiful Cemetery grounds, and just under a low hill where the left of our lines joined the centre. It was in a secluded location, but, as was subsequently proved, in one of the most exposed positions on the extended field of operations. How exposed to shot and shell was the gallant Commander-in-Chief and the brilliant staff which calmly shared his dangers, may be best ascertained by the following vivid description of the correspondent of a New York journal, who himself remained within the building throughout the terrible cannonade. He says :

"In the shadow cast by the tiny farm-house, sixteen by twenty, which General Meade had made his head-quarters, lay wearied staff-officers and tired correspondents. There was not wanting to the peacefulness of the scene the singing of a bird, which had a nest in a peach tree within the tiny yard of the white-washed cottage. In the midst of its warbling, a shell screamed over the house, instantly followed by another and another, and in a moment the air was full of the most complete artillery prelude to an infantry battle that was ever exhibited. Every size and form of shell known to British and to American gunnery, shrieked, whirled, moaned, and whistled and wrathfully fluttered over our ground. As many as six in a second, constantly two in a second, bursting and screaming over and around the head-quarters, made a very hell of fire that amazed the oldest officers. They burst in the yard—burst next to the fence on both sides, garnished as usual with the hitched horses of aids and orderlies. The fastened animals reared and plunged with terror. Then one fell, then another—sixteen lay dead and mangled before the fire ceased, still fastened by their halters, which gave the expression of being wickedly tied up to die painfully. These brute victims of a cruel war touched all hearts. Through the midst of the storm of screaming and exploding shells, an ambulance, driven by its frenzied conductors at full speed, presented to all of us the marvellous spectacle of a horse going rapidly on three legs. A hinder one had been shot off at the hock. A shell tore up the little step at the head-quarters cottage, and ripped bags of oats as with a knife. Another soon carried off one of its two pillars. Soon the spherical case burst opposite the open door—another ripped through the low garret. The remaining pillar went almost immediately to the howl of a fixed shot that Whitworth must have made. During this fire the horses at twenty and thirty feet distant were receiving their death, and soldiers in Federal blue were torn to pieces in the road, and died with the peculiar yells that blend the extorted cry of pain with horror and despair. Not an orderly—not an ambulance—not a straggler was to be seen upon the plain swept by this tempest of orchestral death, thirty minutes after it commenced.   Were not one hundred and twenty pieces of artillery trying to cut from the field every battery we had in position to resist their proposed infantry attack, and to sweep away the slight defences behind which our infantry were waiting?   Forty minutes—fifty minutes—counted watches that ran, oh! so languidly!   Shells through the two lower rooms.   A shell into the chimney, that daringly did not explode. Shells in the yard.   The air thicker and fuller and more deafening with the howling and whirring of these infernal missiles. The Chief of Staff struck—Seth Williams—loved and respected through the army, separated from instant death by two inches of space vertically measured.   An aid bored with a fragment of iron through the bone of the arm.   And the time measured on the sluggish watches was one hour and forty minutes."

Amid all these exciting scenes, General Meade did not for a moment forget his self-possession, but issued his orders with as much calmness and composure as he would have done if his gallant men had been upon a dress parade, instead of being engaged in one of the most bloody battles of modern times.   At length it became impossible for his Aids to bear to the different commanders the orders which were indispensable to the successful continuance of the engagement, and a change being necessary, the little half-destroyed building was evacuated, and General Meade established his head-quarters in a little grove at the foot of one of the hills occupied by General Slocum's Corps.

THE REJOICING AT THE VICTORY.

The glorious victory which crowned the gallantry of the veteran heroes of the Army of the Potomac, sent a thrill of joy to every patriotic heart in the loyal States. From thousands of homes in the North and West came the cries of widows and orphans made desolate during that fearful carnage; but with all the despair and anguish at the loss of their own beloved relations, they did not forget to unite their voices with the millions of exultant freemen in the great song of thanksgiving. Pennsylvania was rescued from the invader, and Baltimore and the Federal Capital were saved, and to the brave defenders, with their skilful leader, who, under the direction of the God of battles, had accomplished these results, were accorded the thanks and laudations of a rescued people.

THE CIRCUMSTANCES UNDER WHICH THE BATTLE WAS FOUGHT.

The battle of Gettysburg was fought under circumstances different from those which marked any of the numerous contests which preceded it. The Union forces had been suddenly drawn into it after a long and fatiguing march, many of the regiments not having been enabled even to take an hour's rest before they became engaged ; they had not yet recovered from the shock they experienced at Chancellorsville; and they were naturally somewhat dispirited by a change of commanders at a time when they momentarily expected to meet the enemy. General Meade was necessarily known to all the principal officers, but there were many of the subordinates, and the large bulk of the rank and file, who had heard of him only as an able commander, who had upon various occasions displayed conspicuous gallantry. To General Meade himself the unexpected promotion was a cause of much anxiety, but he had no fear for the future. His long experience in handling troops; his prompt and active, yet always discreet method of conducting operations; his thorough military education; and the veneration and respect which he always succeeded in creating among the men of his command, rendered him the most desirable officer that could have been selected at that critical hour for the leader of the Potomac army. Upon assuming the command, he made no pledges or promises which he might subsequently find difficult to accomplish, but merely recorded his deter-

mination to do a soldier's duty, leaving to an all-controlling
Providence the decision of the contest. He realized to
the fullest extent the magnitude and importance of the
task imposed upon him, and the successful issue of the
three days' conflict at Gettysburg proved the wisdom of
the selection and the superior ability of the brave man
who planned and fought the battle.

WHO PLANNED THE BATTLE.

It has been rumored that to General Hooker was due
the plan of the fight, but no more unfounded statement
was ever concocted or circulated. Although General
Hooker was necessarily aware from the proximity of the
two opposing forces that an engagement was imminent, it
was utterly impossible for him to foresee the exact spot
where it would take place, nor indeed could General
Meade himself know that the quiet little town of Gettysburg was to be the site. He might have imagined that
with one army to the north and the other to the south of
that place, accessible by highways and by-ways from all
directions, thus giving facilities for the concentration of
troops, the conflict would probably occur in its vicinity,
but beyond that no commander, however great his ability,
could have known.

GENERAL MEADE'S CONGRATULATORY AD-
DRESS TO HIS ARMY.

On the fourth of July, and when it was not yet certain
that the enemy would not make another determined stand
within the Pennsylvania border, General Meade issued
the following congratulatory Address to his victorious
troops :

"HEAD-QUARTERS, ARMY OF THE POTOMAC,
"NEAR GETTYSBURG. *July 4th*, 1863.
"The commanding general, in behalf of the country, thanks
the Army of the Potomac, for the glorious result of the recent

operations. Our enemy, superior in numbers, and flushed with the pride of a successful invasion, attempted to overcome or destroy this army. Baffled and defeated, he has now withdrawn from the contest. The privations and fatigues the army has endured, and the heroic courage and gallantry it has displayed, will be matters of history to be ever remembered.

"Our task is not yet accomplished, and the commanding general looks to the army for greater efforts to drive from our soil every vestige of the presence of the invader.

"It is right and proper that we should, on suitable occasions, return our grateful thanks to the Almighty Disposer of events, that, in the goodness of His providence, He has thought fit to give victory to the cause of the just. By command of

"*Major-General* MEADE.

"S. WILLIAMS, *A. A. G.*"

THE FALL OF VICKSBURG.

Three days later he issued the following order announcing the fall of Vicksburg, the intelligence of which was received by the troops with the wildest enthusiasm :

"HEAD-QUARTERS, ARMY OF THE POTOMAC,
"*July 7th*, 1863.

"It is with much satisfaction that the Major-General commanding, announces to the army under his command, that he has received official intelligence that Vicksburg was surrendered by the enemy to General Grant on the fourth instant.

"By command of "*Major-General* MEADE.
"S. F. BARSTOW, *Assistant Adjutant-General.*"

AN ENGLISHMAN'S OPINION OF GENERAL MEADE.

A correspondent of the London Star, writing from Hagerstown, Maryland, after the battle, thus describes the illustrious hero of Gettysburg :

"I was so fortunate as to be personally introduced to General Meade. He was sitting with General French at the United States Hotel. He is a very remarkable-looking man—tall, spare, of a commanding figure and presence, his manner easy and pleasant, but having much dignity. His head is partially bald, and is small and compact, but the forehead is high. He has the late Duke of Wellington class of nose, and his eyes, which have a serious and almost sad expression, are rather sunken, or appear so from the prominence of the curved nasal development. He has a decidedly patrician and distinguished appearance. I had some conversation—and of his recent achievements he spoke in a modest and natural way. He said that he had been 'very fortunate,' but was most especially anxious not to arrogate to himself any credit which he did not deserve. He said that the triumph of the Federal arms was due to the splendid courage of the Union troops, and also to the bad strategy and rash and mad attacks made by the enemy. He said that his health was remarkably good, and that he could bear almost any amount of physical fatigue. What he complained of was the intense mental anxiety occasioned by the great responsibility of his position."

THE PURSUIT OF THE ENEMY—THE FIGHT AT FALLING WATERS.

On the seventh of July, the two preceding days having been devoted to the burial of the dead and the succor of the wounded, General Meade placed his army in motion for Middletown, Maryland, and after a day's rest at that place, continued through the South Mountain passes, and by the twelfth was in front of the enemy, who were in position in front of Williamsport. On the fourteenth, our cavalry advanced on Williamsport, but Lee had crossed the Potomac on the previous night. At Falling Waters, a few miles below, however, the cavalry overtook the rear guard, capturing two guns, three battle-flags and a number of prisoners.

WHY LEE ESCAPED ACROSS THE POTOMAC.

Notwithstanding the general rejoicing at the victory, and the relief experienced at the retreat across the Potomac of Lee and his followers, a few snarling critics indulged in invidious comments upon the escape, and as a part of the history of the brilliant campaign, we republish the following extracts from a private letter written by a prominent officer, in answer to the unjust strictures to which we allude :

"After the battle of Gettysburg, when Lee retreated through the mountain passes, Meade's army was greatly exhausted by three days' fighting and its previous forced marches, and was also greatly reduced in numbers, having lost nearly twenty thousand men, killed, wounded, and missing, saying nothing of stragglers. Directly to pursue Lee through the mountains, in narrow passes, would have enabled him with a strong rear-guard to have held Meade in check till he could have re-assembled his army in the Cumberland Valley, and then thrown his masses on the heads of his columns when he forced his way through, or he could have detained Meade so long in the mountains that he could easily have gotten away with the main portion of his army if he so desired.

"It was plain that if Lee chose to run away no one in pursuit could stop him, and that the only chance was to endeavor to intercept him at Hagerstown, provided he was not retiring as fast as he might have done. The rise in the Potomac favored Meade, who was able to concentrate his army in Lee's vicinity before he had crossed. But Lee was found in a very strong position, with all his artillery placed, and with his whole army behind breastworks, ready to defend or oppose our advance. The great difficulty was that, owing to the character of the country, it was impossible to reconnoitre Lee's position and ascertain what chances of success our attack would have. Had it been practicable to see exactly where Lee was, and for the general-in-chief to have formed a positive judgment on the subject of the probability of success in an attack, General Meade might have sought no advice, or at least might have given it less importance. But in the absence of such precise information, his duty required that before he incurred the hazards of a blind attack, he should submit the question to those who had to execute the work if decided upon. After consultation, the corps commanders decided that the risks incurred would not justify an attack being made until there was some reasonable degree of probability apparent that it would succeed. They based their judgment on the consequences to the cause and country in case our army should be repulsed and eventually defeated, thus losing all the advantages gained at Gettysburg, and placing Lee completely in mastery of the situation. The country, they thought, depended, at this juncture, on the *existence* of the Army of the Potomac. The reports of the demoralization of the enemy were known to be exaggerated, and the desperateness of his condition, if defeated, would tend to make the battle desperate beyond comparison.

"General Meade acted as a prudent man would have done. The question was, should he order a blind attack when ignorant of all essential matters, having therefore no clear view that success was probable against a splendidly-posted, desperate and powerful enemy, when his five corps commanders advised against it, and when to be defeated was to lose all the benefit of the past victory, and to place the North and Washington again at the command of Lee and his army? Had he seen his own way reasonably clear to victory, he should have discarded advice and overruled his subordinates. But no general-in-chief would have a right to imperil so much when his mind was not clear that he would win.

"The next day after the council was spent in making examinations of the enemy's position. They all resulted in showing him in great force and very strongly posted. But having acquired this fuller though not complete knowledge, General Meade, stronger by delay, determined on an attack the day after. That night General Lee escaped, to the surprise of all— a surprise which has had its counterpart more than once during this war. Such was the surprise of Lee himself when Burnside escaped at Fredericksburg and Hooker at Chancellorsville; of Halleck when Beauregard got away at Corinth.

"On one important fact the public are greatly misinformed. It was generally supposed that General Lee's army was crossing during the day which succeeded the council of war, so that only a part of it lay opposed to Meade for some hours. Such is not the case. *Not a man in Lee's army left his lines till after dark.* Had Meade attacked that day, he would have found Lee's whole army in force, ready to receive him.

"Disappointment at the result no one can blame. Indeed, the chief actors, the corps commanders and the general-in-chief, were the most disappointed of all. But dissatisfaction and censure, such as some journals express or hint, seem positively unjust. It is very improbable that an attack upon Lee, in that position, with his numerous artillery crowning the heights and commanding the defiles and roads, could have been successful. But to have authorized such an attack by a general subjected to the responsibilities which belonged to General Meade, after the victory at Gettysburg, it should have been plain and clear that the chances were in favor of success.

"General Meade is in many respects differently situated from those heretofore in command of the Army of the Potomac. He has had no newspaper claqueurs in the camp or out of it. His present post fell to his lot through the wish of his brother soldiers. To no one was his designation to the important station he holds a greater surprise than to himself. Only sense of duty determined him to accept it. He seeks no personal exaltation now. Whenever it is for the interest of the cause that another should take his place, that moment, those who know him are perfectly assured, he will be prepared cheerfully to vacate his position. It is his cherished opinion that personal considerations should be entirely discarded in this momentous contest. All he pretends to, is the character of an honest soldier sincerely trying to do his duty to the best of his ability. Such a man should receive from all good citizens their earnest regard and support.

"We may say this because we find some are ready to blame

and decry General Meade, notwithstanding his wonderful success.

"It seems to us that in General Meade more desiderata combine than in any former leader of the Army of the Potomac. Of mature age, and with a previous experience which all others lacked, a thoroughly educated soldier, a man of lofty character, loyal to the core, yet unknown to party cliques, embarrassed by no military jealousies, prompt, active, untiring, yet discreet, displaying skill as a field-officer hitherto unprecedented, a soldier and only a soldier, and exhibiting in his despatches and official conduct a modesty and a sense of duty as rare as commendable, we cannot help hoping much from him, and are willing to trust much to him; especially as there looks out from all his conduct one quality in which he stands alone, a humble recognition that victory is of the Lord, and that to Him belongs its glory."

The Army of the Potomac soon after the escape of Lee crossed into Virginia, and resumed its old position on the Rappahannock.

GENERAL MEADE PRESENTED BY THE PENNSYLVANIA RESERVES WITH A HANDSOME TESTIMONIAL.

On the twenty-eighth of August, 1863, the officers of the Pennsylvania Reserve Corps, desirous of presenting him with a testimonial of their esteem and admiration for his talents and skill as an officer and leader, and of their affection for him as a tried friend and courteous gentleman, offered for his acceptance a costly sword of most exquisite workmanship, and accompanied by a sash, belt and pair of golden spurs. The blade of the sword was of the finest Damascus steel, and the scabbard of pure gold, having among the inscriptions the following:

"Mechanicsville, Gaines' Hill, New Market Crossroads, Malvern Hill, Bull Run (Second), South Mountain, Antietam, Fredericksburg, Chancellorsville, Gettysburg."

Near the hilt, inlaid in blue enamel and gold, with precious diamonds, were the initials of General Meade, "G. G. M.;" and the handle of the weapon was encircled with a row of opals, amethysts, rubies and other precious jewels. Invitations were extended to Governor Curtin of Pennsylvania, and a number of gentlemen prominent in civil and military life, who were also present. General S. Wylie Crawford, the gallant commander of the Reserves, was designated as the most suitable person to present the well-deserved tribute, and ably fulfilled the pleasant duty in the following words:

GENERAL CRAWFORD'S PRESENTATION SPEECH.

"GENERAL: I stand before you to-day, sir, the representative of the officers of that division who once called you its chief.

"Impelled by a desire to perpetuate the memory of your connection with them; desirous, too, to manifest to you the affection and esteem they bear to you, they ask the acceptance, to-day, of this testimonial, which shall mark it forever. Accept it, sir, from them, and here, in the presence of him who conceived the idea of this division—and who, I trust, a faithful people will return to the position he so worthily occupies—not as a reward, not as a recompense for your care for them, but as the exponent of those feelings of their hearts whose value cannot be expressed in words. Transmit it to those who bear your name, and let it ever express to you and them that devoted attachment and regard that the officers of the Pennsylvania Reserve corps shall never cease to feel for you."

General Meade then stepped forward amid the most vociferous cheering, and responded as follows:

SPEECH OF MAJOR-GENERAL MEADE.

"*General Crawford and Officers of the Division of the Pennsylvania Reserve Corps:* I accept this sword with feelings of profound gratitude. I should be insensible to all the promptings of nature if I were not grateful and proud at receiving a testimonial of approbation from a band of officers and men so distinguished as has been the division of the Pennsylvania Reserves corps during the whole period of this war. I have a right, therefore, to be proud that they should think my conduct and my course have been of such a character as to justify them in collecting together here so many distinguished gentlemen as I see around me from different parts of the country, and our own State, to present to me this handsome testimonial. It in effect says to me that in their judgment I have done my duty towards them and towards the country. [Applause.] I began my career in this army by commanding the Second brigade of your division. I faithfully endeavored during all the time I held that command, and also the command of your division, to treat the officers and men in a manner that would express to them my high appreciation of their conduct as soldiers and brave men.

"I am very glad, sir, that you have mentioned your distinguished guest, the Governor of Pennsylvania. [Cheers.] I have a personal knowledge of his patriotic efforts in behalf of the soldiers. To him the country is indebted for putting into the field in its hour of sorest need this splendid corps, and I have watched with pleasure and satisfaction the solicitude he has always shown to see that all its interests and wants are attended to. I have been with him on the occasions when he has visited the officers and men from our State, and I know that they are indebted to him for many comforts, and that the country is indebted to him for words of eloquence which he addressed to them to inspire them with increased patriotism and courage. [Cheers.] I am gratified that he is here to witness this presentation, and I heartily join with you, sir, in the hope that his fellow-citizens will remember on election day his services in promoting the interests of the country and the suppression of the rebellion. [Long continued applause.] In speaking of the pride which I experience in receiving this sword, I feel myself justified, even at the risk of being charged with egotism, in saying a few words about the services rendered by this division. I say unhesitatingly here before this assembly, and I am quite sure that when the history of the war is written that the facts will vindicate me, that no division in this glorious army of the Potomac—glorious as I conceive it to be—is entitled to claim more credit for its uniform gallant conduct and for the amount of hard fighting it has gone through than the division of the Pennsylvania Reserve corps. [Cheers.] I do not wish to take any credit to myself in this. It is not of my own personal services that I would speak, but of the services of the soldiers— of the privates of the Pennsylvania Reserve corps, [cheers], and I have only to appeal to Drainesville, where the first success that crowned the arms of the Army of the Potomac was gained, unaided and alone, by a single brigade of the Pennsylvania Reserves. [Cheers.] I have only to refer to Mechanicsville, where began the six days' fighting on the Peninsula, and where the whole of Longstreet's corps was held in check for several hours, and victory really won, by only two brigades of the Reserves. [Cheers.] I refer you to New Market Cross roads, sometimes called Glendale, and refer emphatically to that battle because certain officers of the army, not knowing the true facts of the case, and misled at the time by the statements of others equally ignorant with themselves, and whose statements have since been proved incorrect, brought charges against this division on that occasion. I was with the division during the whole fight, and until dark, when it pleased God that

3

I should be shot down and carried off the field. I have been told that the division ran off, but I know that I stayed with it until it was dark, and my men were engaged in a hand-to-hand contest over the batteries with the enemy. [Cheers.] I do not say that there were not some who ran away, but that is nothing singular. There are cowards in every division; there are bad men in every corps. I do say, however, that the large body of the gallant men of the Pennsylvania Reserves remained on the field until dark, and did not leave it until the enemy had retired. Those guns were never captured from them. [Loud cheers.] They remained on the field, and were not taken until ten o'clock the next day. I refer to South Mountain, and it is not necessary for me to say much of their conduct there, for their gallant ascent of the height in the face of the enemy and turning their left flank was witnessed by the commanding general, and they received full credit for it. [Cheers.] I speak of Antietam, where, on the sixteenth of September, the Pennsylvania Reserve corps, always in the advance, boldly attacked that portion of the Confederate army in its front without knowing its strength, and continued to drive it until dark, and then held the position it had gained until the morning, when the battle was renewed. [Cheers.] I speak again of Fredericksburg, where the Pennsylvania Reserve corps crossed and led the advance, unaided and alone, up the heights, and held their position for half an hour while the others crossed. Had they been followed and supported by other troops, their courage that day would have won a victory. [Cheers.] I repeat, therefore, that I have a right to be proud and grateful when the officers and men of such a command, who can with truth point to a hard-earned and dearly bought record of bright deeds, present me, who have had the honor of commanding them, with such a testimonial. [Applause.] While, however, I give expression to these feelings, they are not unmingled with others of a sad and mournful nature as I look around you and reflect that so many of the brave officers and soldiers who originally composed this division sleep their last sleep, and that others have been obliged to return home crippled and maimed for life. It is terrible to think that there should be any necessity for so much misfortune and misery! Sad, that in this country, a land flowing with milk and honey, and in which we are all brothers, we should raise our arms against each other, and such scenes should be enacted as I have been a participant in. It is sad that there should be an occasion like the present, and a necessity for the presentation of a testimonial such as this. These are sad, sad thoughts to me, but at the same time I am sustained in my present position by a consciousness that I am acting from a high and proper sense of my duty to my country. [Cheers.] It is impossible that this great country should be divided; that there should be two governments or two flags on this continent, such a thing is entirely out of the question. [Cheers.] I trust that every loyal man would be willing to sacrifice his life before he would consent to have more than one government and one flag wave over the whole territory of the United States. [Loud applause.] This reunion, gentlemen, awakens in my heart new sorrow for an officer which it vividly recalls to my mind, for he commanded the division when I commanded one of the brigades. He was the noblest as well as the bravest gentleman in the army. I refer to John F. Reynolds. [Cheers.] I cannot receive this sword without thinking of that officer. When he fell at Gettysburg, leading the advance, I lost not only a lieutenant of the utmost importance to me, but I may say that I lost a friend, aye, even a brother. [Cheers.] I miss other faces which were familiar to me in your midst—McNeil and Taylor, of the Rifles ; Simmons, of the Fifth ; young Kuhn, who came from Philadelphia to assist me in the field ; Dehone, of Massachusetts, and a host of others whose remains you all cherish.

"It is oppressive, gentlemen, to me to go over the list of these officers who have been sacrificed ; but if I could remember and name every soldier of your division that has fallen, what a long list and what a trying recital it would be to us all ! How many men who once belonged to the Pennsylvania Reserve corps now sleep in the grave, or are lingering on earth, joyfully expecting death to end their sufferings.

"I thank you, General Crawford, for the kind manner in which you have conveyed to me this elegant testimonial, and I also thank these gentlemen who have come so far to be present. I trust, sir, this sword will be required but a short time longer. Affairs and events now look as if this unhappy war might be brought to a happy termination. I have to request of you gentlemen who are in civil life that, when you return home, you will spare no efforts to make the people understand that all we want are men to fill up our ranks. Send these to us. Give us the numbers, and the war will soon be concluded. I think the rebels are now satisfied that their struggle is only a matter of time, as we have the force on our side, and that as soon as they see that we are bringing out that force in earnest they will yield. Permit me, before I close, to mention what I intended to refer to before this, but it escaped my memory. I intended to express my delight, sir, on hearing that at Gettysburg, under your command, the Reserve corps enacted deeds worthy of their former reputation, showing that they had lost none of their daring, and could always be relied on in the hour and post of danger. I expected that this would be the case, but it was particularly gratifying to me to hear it from your immediate commander on that occasion. Thanking you for your gallantry there, and again thanking you for your kindness, I will conclude."

REMARKS OF GOVERNOR CURTIN, OF PENN-SYLVANIA.

Governor Curtin, in a few eloquent remarks, bore testimony to the worth and ability of the fearless commander of the Army of the Potomac. He said:

"I am present on an occasion when it has been the pleasure of the officers of this camp, acting upon a plan long since suggested, to present a testimonial to their great and gallant leader, justly deserved by his conduct on the field, and a fit expression of the attachment of the officers and men of this corps to him, called, as he has been, to discharge duties of a higher and more enlarged character.

"To General Meade, allow me to say: The people of Pennsylvania have not been insensible to your military career. You won the confidence of this corps as a brigade commander. You confirmed and enlarged that confidence as a commander of division. The battles before Richmond and gallant conduct in the battles in Maryland fully attest that; and as a commander of corps you obtained the confidence, respect, and love of these gallant men by your conduct at Fredericksburg and the crowning glory of your military life at the great battle of Gettysburg. Recent events prove that this unnatural war, as the general has said, is drawing to a close. I congratulate you on the fact. That rebel army that had the temerity to come upon the sacred soil dedicated to freedom, to poison the air given by God to be breathed by freemen alone, was broken and scattered at Gettysburg. And now, general, as the representative head of the government of your native State, I tender to you the profound gratitude and respect of your fellow-citizens."

SUBSEQUENT MOVEMENTS OF THE CONTEND-ING FORCES—THE FIGHT AT BRISTOE.

But few movements of importance were made by the Army of the Potomac until the early part of October, 1863. On the ninth of that month, the contending forces occupied opposite banks of the Rapidan river, our line extending from Falmouth on the left to Robertson's and Hazel rivers, beyond Thoroughfare Mountain on the right, the centre being in front of Culpeper Court House, and on the same day it was discovered that the enemy had commenced advancing northward. Having satisfied himself by cavalry reconnoissances that Lee was actually moving, the Army of the Potomac was withdrawn to the northern bank of the Rappahannock, but on the following morning, Monday the twelfth, General Meade, for the purpose of ascertaining the true extent of the rebel demonstration, sent the Second, Third and Sixth corps back across the river. The object of their mission was successfully accomplished, and that night they returned to their encampments. In the meantime Lee had advanced from Madison Court House to Sperryville, and on Monday night crossed the Hedgeman river. On Tuesday both armies were pushing forward on parallel lines, when General Lee, upon arriving at Warrenton, formed the bold design of sending a portion of his troops to seize the heights of Centreville, while the remainder fell upon our flank and rear, and by a sudden and determined attack rout our army. But General Meade was too old a soldier to be thus entrapped, and by his superior strategy circumvented the plans of his opponent.

On the fourteenth, the Second Corps under General Warren reached Bristoe Station, on the line of the Alexandria and Orange Railroad, where they found Hill's corps drawn up in line of battle. The troops which had advanced on the left of the railroad, were moved rapidly over to the right, and the cut and embankment which Hill had neglected to occupy, were taken possession of. General Warren hastily formed his troops under cover of the cut and embankment, which constituted natural breastworks. The enemy made an impetuous charge upon his left flank, when the heroes rose from their cover, and at close range poured volley after volley into the ranks of the advancing foe. A short but severe engagement followed, resulting in the signal repulse of the rebels, who fled from the field, leaving their dead and wounded, several hundred prisoners, and seven guns. Ten men from each regiment engaged were detailed to bring in the pieces, and in the attempt they were attacked by the former owners, who succeeded in recovering two of the guns. Other but less important engagements took place during the week, and after the destruction by Lee of several miles of railroad, that General, convinced of the impossibility of outwitting the Union Commander, commenced a retrograde movement, and returned across the Rappahannock, closely pursued by the Army of the Potomac. The rebels continuing their retreat until the Rapidan had been passed, further pursuit was necessarily suspended. During this brief campaign, General Meade endeavored repeatedly to bring on a general engagement, but Lee did not desire such a conflict and carefully avoided it.

BRILLIANT ENGAGEMENTS ON THE RAPPA-HANNOCK.

During the interval which elapsed between the fight at Bristoe Station and the seventh of November, several important cavalry reconnoissances were made, but on that day two severe and brilliant engagements took place on the Rappahannock. The rebels had intrenched themselves on the Southern bank of that stream, and deeming themselves secure from interference, had commenced the construction of huts with the expectation of remaining in their position during the winter months. To their surprise, however, on the morning of the seventh, a movement of the army was made under the personal superintendence of General Meade. Moving in two columns, the right, comprising the Fifth and Sixth Corps, under the command of General Sedgwick, advanced towards Rappahannock Station, and the left, comprising the First, Second and Third Corps, under command of General French, to Kelly's Ford. At an early hour of the afternoon, General Sedgwick arrived before the enemy's works at Rappahannock, and driving the skirmishers before them, occupied a crest less than a mile distant, and posted his guns. An artillery fire soon commenced, and during its progress a storming party consisting of four regiments of General Russell's Brigade and

two of Colonel Upton's Brigade, was organized, and with
a cheer which appalled the enemy, made a determined
assault upon the forts and rifle-pits. To reach the works
a half-mile of open plain had to be traversed, and deep
ditches to be crossed, but regardless of the mark they
presented to the enemy while dashing over the one, and
of the difficulties offered in crossing the other, they moved
steadily forward without expending a single shot upon
their assailants. At a double-quick advanced this gallant
band, and not until the ramparts had been reached, was a
single musket discharged. A desperate hand-to-hand
struggle for mastery continued for twenty minutes, resulting in victory to our troops, and the surrender of the
enemy. Four guns and about two thousand stand of arms
were captured, and about sixteen hundred of their officers
and men taken prisoners. The column which had moved
on Kelly's Ford, after a brief but warm engagement, were
also successful, the rifle-pits being captured and a large
number of their defenders having thrown down their arms
and surrendered. On the following morning it was discovered that the rebels had evacuated their positions
during the night, and pursuit was immediately ordered
and continued to Brandy Station, a short distance this
side of Culpeper Court-House.

GENERAL MEADE'S CONGRATULATORY
ORDER.

General Meade subsequently issued the following congratulatory order:

"HEAD-QUARTERS, ARMY OF POTOMAC,
"*November 9th,* 1863.

"The commanding general congratulates the army upon the
recent successful passage of the Rappahannock in the face of
the enemy, compelling him to withdraw to his intrenchments
behind the Rapidan. To Major-General Sedgwick and the
officers and men of the Sixth and Fifth corps participating in
the attack, particularly the storming party under Brigadier-

General Russell, his thanks are due for the gallantry displayed in the assault on the enemy's intrenched position of Rappahannock Station, resulting in the capture of four guns, two thousand small arms, eight battle-flags, one bridge train, and sixteen hundred prisoners. To Major-General French and the officers and men of the corps that were engaged, particularly to the leading column, commanded by Colonel D. E. Frobey, his thanks are due for the gallantry displayed in the crossing at Kelly's Ford, and seizure of the enemy's intrenchments, and the capture of over four hundred prisoners. The commanding general takes great pleasure in announcing to the army that the President has expressed his satisfaction with its recent operations.

" By command of   " GEORGE G. MEADE,
                                         " Major-General.
" (Signed)   " S. WILLIAMS, A. A. G."

HIS ADDRESS TO THE SIXTH CORPS.

On the afternoon of the tenth, Colonel Upton, who commanded a portion of the troops who had so successfully charged and captured the enemy's works at Rappahannock Station, presented General Meade with the eight battle-flags taken at that time. Colonel Upton presented the flags in the name of the command, when General Meade responded as follows:

" Colonel Upton, officers and men of the Sixth corps :—I receive, with great satisfaction, the battle-flags as evidences of the good conduct and gallantry you displayed on the seventh instant. The assault on the enemy's position at Rappahannock Station, intrenched by redoubts and rifle-pits, and defended by artillery and infantry, carried, as it was, at the point of the bayonet, was a work which could only have been executed by the best of soldiers, and in the result of which you may be justly proud. It gives me great confidence that, in future operations, I can implicitly rely on the men under my command doing all that men can do ; and, although it is my desire to place you in such positions as to avoid the possible recurrence of such contests, yet there are occasions, such as the recent ones, when it is the only and the best course to pursue. And to feel, as I do now, that I command men able and willing to meet and overcome such obstacles, is a source of great satisfaction. I shall transmit these flags to the War Department. I have already reported your good conduct, and received and transmitted to your commanders the approval of the President. I shall prepare (as soon as I receive the requisite information) a general order, in which it is my desire to do justice to all the troops who have distinguished themselves; and it is my purpose, by every means in my power, to have those soldiers rewarded who have merited such distinction. Soldiers, in the name of the army and the country I thank you for the services you have rendered, particularly for the example you have set, which I doubt not, on future occasions, will be followed and emulated."

LOCUST GROVE AND MINE RUN—GENERAL MEADE'S RESPONSIBLE POSITION.

On the morning of the twenty-sixth of November, 1863, General Meade again placed his army in motion, with the design of attacking the enemy and forcing him to evacuate his line of defence, with the expectation of severing his forces and beating them in detail. The plan was well-devised, but was frustrated by untoward fortune. The enemy had unfortunately become early informed of the movement, and had prepared themselves for the contest. On the twenty-seventh was fought the battle of Locust Grove, resulting in the success of our troops and the retreat of the enemy, with heavy loss. On the twenty-eighth they were pursued towards their defences on the west bank of Mine Run, a small tributary of the Rapidan. During that night the rebels worked industriously, strengthening their intrenchments. The position was indeed one of rare strength, the line being formed on a series of ridges with enfilading positions for batteries, while in front stretched an extensive marsh. General Warren carefully reconnoitered the enemy's right, and reported the practicability of success, but on examining carefully, General Meade concluded he could not carry it without a fearful sacrifice of life. On the morning of Monday, the thirtieth, our artillery opened upon the works, but after an hour or two of constant firing, the bombardment ceased. A retrograde movement was decided upon, and by the third of December the army was again back in its old position near Brandy Station. The propriety of the advance and the necessity of the return were duly discussed by the military critics, but the vast majority of the people of the country experienced renewed confidence in the commander who had had sufficient moral courage to relinquish a movement, and retire from a conflict, in preference to heeding the popular clamor for an advance. General Meade knew the great responsibility which rested upon him. Success, even if his efforts were so rewarded, could but have been secured at an immense sacrifice, and with but slight ultimate advantage to the army or the cause. Upon the other hand, defeat would have been most disastrous, affording Lee facilities for the accomplishment of the darling project of the Southern people, the capture of the Capital of the Union, which neither the conquered army of Meade, nor the freemen of the North, who might have hastened to the rescue, could have prevented. The occupation of Washington would have been but temporary, but the disgrace resulting from such possession would have been most humiliating. Just previous to the movement, General Meade, in a letter to a friend, thus referred to his plans :

"I am fully aware of the great anxiety in the public mind that something should be done. I am in receipt of many letters, some from persons in high position, telling me I had better have my army destroyed and the country filled up with the bodies of the soldiers than remain inactive. Whilst I do not suffer myself to be influenced by such communications, I am and have been most anxious to effect something, but am determined, at every hazard, not to attempt any thing unless my judgment indicates a probability of accomplishing some object commensurate with the destruction of life necessarily involved. I would rather, a thousand times, be relieved, charged with tardiness or incompetency, than have my conscience burdened with a wanton slaughter, uselessly, of brave men, or with having jeopardized the great cause by doing what I thought wrong."

GENERAL MEADE IN PHILADELPHIA — ADDRESSES THE CONVALESCENT SOLDIERS AND THE UNION LEAGUE.

Early in January, 1864, General Meade visited Philadelphia on a brief leave of absence, but when about to re-

turn, was suddenly taken with an attack of illness brought
on by continued exposure, which, increasing in severity,
confined him for some time to his bed. On the thirteenth
of the same month, and before he had regained his health,
he was honored with a complimentary serenade, tendered
him by a number of soldiers, convalescent inmates of one
of the Army sanitary institutions of Philadelphia. After
the Band had ceased playing a national air, General Meade
came forward and made the following address :

"*Fellow Soldiers :*—Those of you belonging to the Army of
the Potomac who are from the field of Gettysburg, as many of
you doubtless are, need no light to recognize my voice and my
features. I am delighted to see you here, and glad to see that
you have so far recovered from your wounds that you are able
to march out on this inclement night. And I am gratified that
the soldiers of my old command should visit me and extend me
such a welcome. We are anxious for your entire and speedy
recovery. I have just left the army, where I must soon return.
There all your old comrades are re-enlisting, anxious to remain
in the army until they bring this unnatural and unholy war to a
termination : a termination which shall be satisfactory to us ; a
termination which will be worthy of the old flag, and an honor
to the government. And this must be the re-establishment of
the old Union in its former glory, and the acknowledgment of
the Constitution from one end of this continent to the other.
I am glad to see that you are all so well, and able to leave your
quarters to-night. I hope to find you soon in the ranks, where
I am obliged to return. We are making every effort to improve
the present, and, as soon as the weather moderates, and the
season will allow, active operations will be commenced anew,
and in earnest. We want you all to be there. We want you
all to return, and to bring all you can with you ; and may you
all live to see what we all want to see, this struggle brought to
a speedy and a glorious end. It is a question of numbers and
of time. You all know that, if we but bring the men to the work,
it will be ended speedily. I have nothing further to say, except
that I return you my thanks for the welcome you have this
night extended me."

A SECOND SERENADE.

The Union League assembled at their rooms later in the
evening, and, preceded by a band, marched to the house
where the General was stopping. The whole street was
closed with the people who accompanied the League;

and, in response to repeated calls, the General appeared and made the following remarks:

"I am much obliged to you, my friends, for your compliment in giving three cheers for Gettysburg. I am here but for a very few days, and have only visited my home to see my wife and children, and I am happy to hear you remember Gettysburg and its deeds of heroic daring. I speak to Philadelphians; I have always felt it to be a matter of pride that I am a Philadelphian. Every thing that I do in the discharge of my duties is increased and nerved with new strength when I think that I am a Philadelphian, and that my fellow-citizens of Philadelphia will be glad to hear, when I come back among them, that I have done my duty. As I said when I took command of the Army of the Potomac, I say to you now. I have no pledges to make. When I return to my army, all I can say is that we will do the best we can to suppress the rebellion and to overthrow all those who are in arms against our common country; and we will do the best we can to have our flag respected, and to have it wave over every foot of ground from the Canadas to the Rio Grande, and the golden sands of the Pacific. The banner of the stars and bars we will number among the things of the past, and the rebellion, with all its associations, will be remembered as things that have existed, but have no longer any being. What we need is men. I want you here, all of you, every man of you, however small may be his influence, to use that influence to send recruits to the army. The more we get the better will it be for that army, and the quicker will the war be ended. The war must be ended by hard fighting, and it becomes every man, woman, and child to work for the increase of our armies in the field; and, when that is done, I trust that next summer will come to us with peace restored to the land, and happiness, contentment, and prosperity pervading the entire country."

GENERAL MEADE AND THE PHILADELPHIA COUNCILS.

Two days later, the Councils of the City of Philadelphia adopted the following resolution:

"Appreciating the patriotism and military skill of Major-General Meade, and the brilliant victory obtained over the rebel army at Gettysburg, by the glorious Army of the Potomac, under his command, it is the desire of the Councils to give the citizens of Philadelphia an opportunity to testify to him their grateful sense of the importance of the victory of Gettysburg, by a personal interview with him. It is therefore

"*Resolved,* That Councils, through the Presidents of their respective chambers, invite General Meade to meet the Councils and the citizens of Philadelphia in Independence Hall, at such time as may be convenient to him, and that the Mayor of the city be requested to welcome him to the city of Philadelphia."

Another resolution was also adopted, appropriating one thousand dollars for the purchase of a sword, to be presented to General Meade.

HE IS THANKED BY CONGRESS.

Subsequently, a joint resolution was passed by Congress, expressing the gratitude of the American people, and tendering the thanks of their representatives in Congress to General Meade, for his skill and heroic valor as displayed at Gettysburg.

HIS PUBLIC RECEPTION IN PHILADELPHIA—ENTHUSIASTIC DEMONSTRATION.

On the ninth of February, 1864, the hero of Gettysburg having recovered sufficiently to allow him to conform to the unanimous wish of his fellow-citizens, and thus give them an opportunity to manifest their esteem and regard for him as a man, and their confidence in him as a military leader, he received a most gratifying and enthusiastic reception. Upon his arrival at Independence Hall, he was greeted with the most vociferous cheering by the assembled multitude. In the Hall were assembled the members of the Councils and other officials, civil and military, and after being introduced to the Mayor, he was welcomed by that officer in the following chaste address :

MAYOR HENRY'S SPEECH.

"General : Your visit to the City. although alone intended for the endearments of home, has afforded to your fellow-citizens an opportunity for the public recognition of your signal services, and for expression of the grateful esteem in which you are justly held. For this purpose the Councils of Philadelphia have invited you to the Hall of Independence, and in their name I bid you the welcome that is due to every champion in our country's cause, but to none so fitly as the successful defender of the State within which this venerated edifice is reared. Such civic testimonial of respect can but inadequately evince the gratitude of this community towards the able leader and the intrepid soldiers of the Army of the Potomac—that Army before whose conceded prowess the foe quailed with instinctive dread as they confronted its firm ranks upon the glorious heights of Gettysburg. Twice in our country's annals has the Fourth day of July been of special note. The presence in which you stand, and the memorials which surround you, tell of the earlier day when the inspiration of patriots gave forth from this Hall that grand creed for all humanity, whose truths, passing the comprehension of their teachers, are at length, after three generations of unbelief, finding acceptance through the baptism of blood as the vital, essential tenets for our national perpetuity.

"To the memorable hours of the later anniversary, the gratitude of those who now greet you can bear ready witness. The remembrance is still fresh of that joy which filled every loyal heart, and beamed from every loyal eye, a joy almost too great for belief or utterance, when the morning of that day brought the glad certainty that the rebel invaders had been overthrown, and that their broken columns were fleeing in dismay from the soil which had been polluted by their tread. Memory can yet vividly recall the fervent thanks which ascended to the Giver of all victory, and the rich benisons that were invoked from His hand upon the brave defenders of our State. No untoward fortunes or ungrateful devices can rob you of the proud distinction that was then acquired, or can cancel the enduring obligations of our country to the gallant army that under your leadership gained new renown in the hard-won conflicts of Gettysburg.

"In returning to the arduous duties of your high command, bear with you the assurance of the hearty confidence of your fellow-citizens of Philadelphia, and of the special interest with which they must ever view each success you shall achieve in advancing your country's flag. Carry also with you the self-evident truth that not one sinew of this people has been weakened or over-strained in their gigantic efforts to maintain their just cause. After three years of incessant warfare, there is to-day no less determination to preserve this Union ; no less ability to effect that purpose, and no less faith in its sure result, than when rebellion first bid defiance to the Federal power.

"Again, General, I offer the cordial congratulations of your fellow-citizens, and their earnest wishes for your undimmed prosperity and honors."

REPLY OF GENERAL MEADE.

General Meade then, in a modest, unassuming manner, sincerely thanked the Mayor, members of Councils and citizens of Philadelphia for the distinguished honor conferred upon him. He hardly knew how to give utterance to his feelings for the ovation extended. When he came to Philadelphia to visit his family, he had no thought that he would be called upon to witness such a demonstration. He thanked the citizens, through their representatives, for this reception. Sometimes he thinks that too much importance is attached to his humble efforts in behalf of the Union. To his officers, brigade commanders, regimental commanders, and company commanders, but more particularly to the heroic bearing of the private soldiers, the great success of the army is due. If he had not the support of his soldiers, not all the military skill in the world could succeed. He desired that the credit should be given to his army. After the Battle of Gettysburg, he fully appreciated the services of that army which is sometimes called unfortunate. When the record of that army becomes fully known, it will appear that that army is one of the most gallant and determined that the world ever saw. As a statistical fact, he would state that since March, 1861, not less than one hundred thousand men had been killed and wounded. He thought that record would show what that army has done. When the season for operations commences, it will be his duty to again lead that army to the field, and he will feel greatly inspired when he knows that his efforts are appreciated. The General concluded his remarks by again returning thanks for the reception.

The members of Councils were then severally introduced to the General by the respective Presidents of the two branches, and the doors being thrown open, an immense throng pressed forward. For an hour he was engaged in shaking hands with his patriotic fellow-citizens, when the crowd increasing rather than diminishing, it was deemed advisable to dispense with the hand-shaking, and the General subsequently returned the attention of his admirers by bowing to them, as they saluted him as they passed.

IS APPOINTED BRIGADIER-GENERAL IN THE REGULAR ARMY.

General Meade almost immediately afterwards returned

to his head-quarters in the field, and on the twenty-ninth of February, 1864, was confirmed by the Senate as Brigadier-General in the Regular army, his commission to date from July 3d, 1863.

General Meade is but one of a large family, the members of which are identified with the Union service. His eldest son, George, is connected with his staff, with the rank of Captain; his brother-in-law, Colonel Hartman Bache, is a distinguished officer of the Engineers; another brother-in-law, William Sergeant, and a nephew, A. J. Dallas, are Captains in the Twelfth Regular Infantry; his brother, Richard W. Meade, is a Captain in the Navy; two sons of this brother are also in the Navy, and a third in the Marine Corps, a gallant relative who was captured by the enemy in the celebrated night attack upon Fort Sumter, and is now a prisoner in Columbia, South Carolina; and another nephew, a son of Colonel Hartman Bache, is a member of his staff.

General Meade was married on the last day of December, 1840, to a daughter of the Hon. John Sergeant, of Philadelphia, and has four sons and three daughters.

Few officers are more devoted to their country than the subject of our sketch, and few have evinced that devotion in a more satisfactory and honorable manner. His promotion has been rapid, but at the same time sufficiently delayed to enable him to become acquainted with his troops, and to train them for the future accomplishment of deeds of valor which have been unsurpassed in their brilliancy. The soldiers adore him, the country has confidence in him, and the enemy fear him. What better promise of success could we have than with such a commander?

THE END.

THE LIFE, CAMPAIGNS, AND SERVICES

OF

GENERAL McCLELLAN.

THE HERO OF WESTERN VIRGINIA! SOUTH MOUNTAIN! AND ANTIETAM!

With a full history of his Campaigns, and Battles, and his Reports and Correspondence with the War Department and the President in relation to them, from the time he first took the field in this war, until he was finally relieved from command after the Battle of Antietam.

Philadelphia:
T. B. PETERSON & BROTHERS, 306 CHESTNUT STREET.

PRICE 50 CENTS.

General Grant's Life and Public Services.

THE LIFE AND SERVICES AS A SOLDIER

OF

MAJOR-GENERAL GRANT.

EVERY PERSON SHOULD READ THIS LIFE OF GENERAL GRANT.

HERO OF FORT DONELSON! VICKSBURG! AND CHATTANOOGA!

Commander of the Military Division of the Mississippi; and Captor of 472 Cannon and over 90,000 Rebel Prisoners.

Philadelphia:

T. B. PETERSON & BROTHERS, 306 CHESTNUT STREET.

PRICE 25 CENTS.

www.ingramcontent.com/pod-product-compliance
Lightning Source LLC
Chambersburg PA
CBHW021225260626
47172CB00002B/601